A Flight of
Dazzle Angels

········•────◆───•········

WILLIAM H. HOOKS

Macmillan Publishing Company
New York

Macmillan Publishing Company, 866 Third Avenue, New York, NY 10022
Collier Macmillan Canada, Inc.

First Edition   Printed in the United States of America

10 9 8 7 6 5 4 3 2 1

The text of this book is set in 11½ point Bembo.
Library of Congress Cataloging-in-Publication Data
Hooks, William H. A flight of dazzle angels / William H. Hooks. — 1st
ed.   p.   cm. Summary: In a small southern town in 1908, fifteen-year-old Annie Earle, though afflicted with a club foot and surrounded by a sick mother and brother, gains a new insight into herself and the possibilities of her life through her relation-ship with a young black woman and a new young man in town with whom she falls in love.
ISBN 0–02–744430–9
[1. Physically handicapped—Fiction. 2. Family problems—Fiction. 3. Friendship—Fiction. 4. Race relations—Fiction. 5. Southern States—Fiction.
I. Title. PZ7.H7664F1 1988   [Fic]—dc19   88–11993 CIP AC

For Candy, Jeff, William, and Molly

Contents

Annie Earle and Brodie Lacewell

A nnie Earle was perched stonelike on the edge of the front steps, next to a clump of azaleas, heavy with pink and lavender blossoms. She was aching to move, but the giant monarch butterfly was a cautious one. It buzzed the nectar-laden flowers with fast thrusts, robbing a bit of sweetness on each pass. *If I don't make a move, he'll get careless. Light long enough for me to make the catch.* She could feel the sun burning right through her long, straight auburn hair. Her cheeks felt fevered, but she didn't stir.

She could see Brodie Lacewell in the cool, deep shadow behind the Virginia creeper vines on the front porch. Even in the shadows Brodie looked pale, pale all over. A shaft of light found its way through the vines and shot through his white curly hair, making it look like a crinkly halo. *I've got it, Brodie. You look just like one of those transparent angels in the altar painting at the Episcopal church.*

The monarch made a landing and dug into a rich nectar cache. One sure, swift swipe and Annie Earle had it cupped in her hands.

"Brodie, stop that nicktating and come see what I got," she called.

Deep in the porch shade, Brodie Lacewell kept staring into space, still as a leaf on a hot, humid, breezeless day.

"Brodie Lacewell! Brodie Lacewell, you're nicktating again!" shouted Annie Earle. "Come see what I got."

Brodie's pale hands fluttered as if they heard. But the angel face of purity lingered in the realm of nicktation.

1

"Come on, Brodie. You gonna make me have to get up and shake you?" asked Annie Earle.

Holding the big orange-and-black butterfly in one hand, Annie Earle pushed against the porch step with the other hand and raised her body to a standing position. With the help of a porch rail, she pulled herself up the steps and started walking toward Brodie. Her clubfoot caused her to dip precariously to the right with every other step. The sound of her heavy shoes on the porch boards made a rhythm—*step-slap, step-slap*.

"Brodie, Brodie, beautiful Brother Brodie, look at the butterfly I caught for you," cooed Annie Earle as she gently shook Brodie Lacewell.

His mouth twitched, and long golden lashes swept across the pale blue eyes, bringing him into Annie Earle's world.

"Look, Brodie. It's a monarch. Took me half an hour pretending to be a statue to get him to light close enough to catch. It's for your collection, Brodie. Do you like it?"

"Beautiful," answered Brodie. "But it's alive."

"That's no problem," replied Annie Earle. "I'll just pinch his head off like this." She severed the head neatly with a quick pinch of her fingernails.

"Stop, Sister Annie Earle! Wait till I get the ether. No, stop!" cried Brodie. Too late.

"Aw, come on, Brodie. I didn't ask *you* to do it. You want a monarch for your collection, don't you? Well, you can't just wait around until one falls dead in your path. Here, take it and put it in a jar so it won't get crushed."

Annie Earle grasped one of Brodie's hands and dropped the butterfly into it.

"It's still trembling," whispered Brodie.

"I assure you, Brodie Lacewell, it doesn't feel a thing.

Now go find a mason jar. You're gonna love this specimen. Just wait till you see it slap-dab in the middle of your display case. This is a centerpiece butterfly if ever I've seen one."

Brodie drifted toward the screen door with the monarch resting in the palm of his open hand.

"What would you do without me, Brodie?" called Annie Earle. As he disappeared into the house, she added, "Don't worry, Brodie. You may be a year older than me, but I'll look after you. Forever."

Annie Earle sat on the porch in the comfortable old rocking chair, pumping rhythmically with her strong left foot. The *click-clock* of the well-worn rocker treads never failed to turn the magical trick. Soon she would be able to rock her way through the dull, nagging pain that had invaded her right foot long ago, put down roots like a tenacious squatter, staking out territory it had no intention of relinquishing. When she had thinking to do, she rocked. The heavier the thinking, the harder the rocking. Today she just might turn her worry rocker upside down to get her thinking straightened out. She rocked furiously.

At first Mama had said she didn't see why Annie Earle would be the least bit interested in going to the school graduation dance. Mama and Annie Earle had gone over it quite thoroughly last night.

"Annie Earle, you're fifteen years old now," said Mama, "and I'm going to treat you like a grown-up lady. We have to face the fact that God has set his mark on our lives. Once we accept that, all our burdens will be lifted."

"Mama, we're talking about a little old school dance, not about God," countered Annie Earle.

"Well, honey, yes, we are," answered Mama. "And

my duty as a parent, and at this point your only parent, is to see after your spiritual and your temporal life. I must protect you and Brodie Lacewell."

"Mama, I've been protected so long, I don't feel like I've done any living yet. I'm stronger than anybody in this family. Including you, Mama. And I just want to be like everybody else."

"Annie Earle Roland, hold your horses. You're driving at a reckless speed. I may be what some folks refer to as an invalid, but I'm your mother. And I've seen what life can do. I've known hurt, Annie Earle, and I want to save my children from as much as possible. That's why I've tried to build a wall of seclusion and protection around you and Brodie Lacewell. Besides, you're not as strong as you claim, baby. That swelling in your bad leg worries me."

"Well, it doesn't worry me much. I'm used to it. And it only happens once in a great while."

"You know what else I'm talking about, Annie Earle."

"No, I don't know what you're talking about, Mama. I really don't. Why don't you want me to go to the dance?"

"Baby, why do you always ask me to cause you pain? Do I have to ask, Can you dance?"

"No, Mama, I can't dance. And you don't cause me pain by asking. But I can watch other people dancing. And enjoy it, too. You should have seen the boys practicing at the school gym. Some of them looked more club-footed than me."

Mama winced at the word.

"And, besides, they need folks to serve the punch. And everyone doesn't dance all the time. They say there's a lot of sitting on the sidelines and talking. And I would love hearing the music, Mama."

"I won't say no," Mama said finally, "but think about

it, Annie Earle. I just don't want you to be hurt. Think about it, and we'll talk again tomorrow."

Annie Earle *was* thinking. And rocking hard. Mama made it a challenge. Annie Earle felt obligated to put up a good front. But behind the good front, in the secret place she kept for herself alone, she was scared.

I'll be the only one there who doesn't dance at least once. What'll I do with my dance card? It's the last chance I'll ever have to go to a school dance. Never been to one yet. Sure would surprise a lot of folks if I turned up. Truth is, I'm scared to go. But I do believe I'm more scared not to go. Annie Earle Roland, you run away from this, you'll end up like Mama, refined and reclining on a pink padded chaise longue and never leaving your bedroom. Or worse, you could drift into nicktating like poor sweet Brodie and bid this real world good-bye.

I've got it, Mama. I've got it. From this day on, I'm stepping out of this gray, secluded world I've been living in. I don't care how many times I fall down. I'm going out there and bloody my knees if I have to. I'm going to that dance! And I'll need a new dress. Not a long one to hide my infirmity. But a short one with the ankles showing. And beads on it, Mama. The latest 1908 style. Annie Earle's going to the dance, Mama, in style!

The rocking chair almost flipped over. "Mama, Mama!" Annie Earle cried as she pulled herself up the stairs to Mama's bedroom. "Mama, I've thought about it. And I'm going to the dance. I'll need a new dress. Aunt Charlotte can make it. I want seed pearls sewn all around the neckline. And scattered on the skirt like stars. Can it be blue? Then the pearls will really look like stars."

"Child, child, I can see that square set of your jaw. Just like your daddy. Your energy leaves me weak. Calm down. You're determined to go?"

"Yes, Mama, I'm going."

Mama rang her little silver bell.

"Let's get Aunt Charlotte here to measure you. Then we'll need to buy material. There's only a week to get it all done. I'm getting too worked up. Hand me my pillbox, Annie Earle. My heart's just a-fluttering."

An old fear grabbed Annie Earle, tempering the excitement she felt. *Mama's pills. Mama's fluttering heart. Mama, the slender thread that keeps us together as a family. Snap!* She closed her mind to it, refusing to think about it, rejecting the idea of bringing Mama's condition to her worry rocker today. She handed Mama the pillbox and hugged her. "Thanks, Mama."

Aunt Charlotte entered the room.

"You ring, Miss Penelope?" she asked Mama.

"Yes, Aunt Charlotte. We need the sewing basket. I want you to measure Annie Earle for a dancing dress. Our Annie Earle's going to her first dance. What do you think of that?"

Aunt Charlotte's brown face beamed broad and bright with a gold-toothed grin. "It's real nice, Miss Penelope. Nothing will do but silk georgette. Right? I'll make her a dress fit for a princess."

"Annie Earle wants seed pearls on it," added Mama.

"Brodie Lacewell can help do that," said Annie. "He's good at sewing things on."

"Lord have mercy!" exclaimed Aunt Charlotte. "This family seems to be getting into high gear again."

Mama sighed heavily. "Everybody go now. That's all the excitement I can stand for one day. My pill's taking effect. Leave me be."

Aunt Charlotte and Annie Earle left the room.

"I ain't seen your mama so excited in years," said Aunt Charlotte.

"It'll be good for Mama," answered Annie Earle.

6

"I think it'll be good for you, too," replied Aunt Charlotte.

"Brodie! Brodie Lacewell!" called Annie.

Brodie appeared at the foot of the stairs.

"I need your help, Brodie!" exclaimed Annie Earle. "You've got to sew dozens of seed pearls on a dance dress for me. And every one of them has to be exactly spaced. Will you do that for me, Brodie?"

"Yes," said Brodie. "I'll do them exactly, Sister Annie. They'll all be spaced exactly. I promise, Sister Annie Earle. I promise."

Queen Esther

·⋯—◆▶—·⋯

It was during the feverish week of making the dress that Aunt Charlotte asked Annie Earle about bringing in her granddaughter. "Queen Esther's just moved back here. And there be so much to do, we need another pair of hands," declared Aunt Charlotte.

Her granddaughter had beautiful hands. They were the first things Annie Earle noticed—light tan on top and pinkish in the palms, with long, delicate fingers ending in mauve fingernails.

"You remember my granddaughter, Queen Esther," said Aunt Charlotte.

"Queen!" exclaimed Annie Earle. "How could I forget Queen Esther? You sure have changed since we used to play together."

Queen Esther dropped her head and smiled. "You looking good," she said. "We both changed a lot. But I never forget you, Annie Earle. All those years we lived over in Clarkton, I never forget. I be glad to see you again."

"Come on," said Aunt Charlotte. "Let's go up and see Miss Nel."

Mama stared at the young girl. "This can't be that little granddaughter who used to come play with Annie Earle. I declare, you close your eyes to sneeze and they're grown up these days. How old are you, Queen Esther?"

"I turned sixteen, ma'am," answered Queen Esther.

"Queen's a good girl, Miss Penelope. And she be a help

8

at anything to do with housework. Queen have knowing hands. Some say she got healing hands."

"Well, hands we need, especially this week to get our Annie Earle ready. It saps my strength just thinking about it. Annie Earle, have you been to Kramer's Department Store for the sample yet?"

"No, Mama. I was about to go when Queen Esther popped in."

"Well, why don't you take Queen Esther with you. While you're getting the dress sample, Queen can pick up some strawberries at the market. I've got such a craving for fresh strawberries."

On the way Queen Esther asked, "Is Miss Penelope sick? And where's Brodie? I didn't see Brodie."

"One at a time, Queen. Brodie was up in his room mounting a new batch of butterflies for his collection. Brodie's the same, doing a lot of nicktating and still scaring the life out of us when he has one of his seizures."

"And Miss Nel?"

"Mama's no sicker than usual."

"I remember her being so lively."

"Oh, that was before Daddy died. Mama's been practically an invalid ever since Daddy passed away. She says the only thing keeps her going is her medicine."

"Can Miss Nel walk?"

"Yes, but she hardly ever leaves her room."

"Well, I'm going to try to find her the sweetest strawberries in town. Sounds like strawberries just might cheer her up."

"Queen, I'm glad you're back."

Annie Earle thumped her way across the front porch and entered the cool, darkened hallway. Queen Esther trailed behind.

"Aunt Charlotte," called Annie Earle, "I got the samples! Come and look!"

Annie Earle met Aunt Charlotte in the parlor, while Queen Esther rushed to the kitchen with the strawberries.

"Sit down, child. You flushed as a sun-ripe tomato," said Aunt Charlotte.

"It's already hot as August out there," said Annie Earle.

"You just excited," replied Aunt Charlotte. "Come on, let's see them samples."

Annie Earle quickly started spreading out the swatches of cloth.

"Mrs. Kramer had three shades of blue silk: this pale one, this medium one, and this deep royal shade. And she sent this blue sample of cotton organdy. It's a lot cheaper." Annie Earle was spreading the last sample on the library table just as Queen Esther returned.

"Which one do you like?" she asked Aunt Charlotte.

Aunt Charlotte studied the strips of cloth. "I do believe pale blue silk be the proper thing for a young girl," she answered.

Queen Esther gently stroked each of the four samples with the tip of her slender index finger. Then she leaned close to Annie Earle and whispered, "Royal blue. Pick the royal blue. It'll change your life. There's power in this color. Pick it."

"What you mumbling about?" asked Aunt Charlotte with slight irritation in her voice.

"I was telling Annie Earle that royal blue is mighty pretty," said Queen Esther.

"Well, Miss Nel's gonna have something to say about it," replied Aunt Charlotte.

"I just know Mama's going to side with Aunt Charlotte and put me in proper pale blue," said Annie Earle. "I really like the deep royal the best."

But to everyone's surprise, Mama took one look at the samples and said, "Nothing will do but royal blue for our Annie Earle. I hope you like it, too, baby, because it's so right."

Annie Earle glanced at Queen Esther, and Queen quickly winked and then turned her head.

"It's settled then?" asked Annie Earle. "I can go back and get the material?"

"Yes," answered Mama. "Tell Mrs. Kramer to put it on my account. And on the way back, stop at Simmons's and refill my pills and the liquid. Just ask Mr. Simmons for both refills. I'll need a good supply to get through this week."

"Come on, Queen," said Aunt Charlotte. "We got to get out the patterns and set up the cutting board. Come on, girls, let's get a move on."

As Annie Earle rushed from the house, she noticed Brodie Lacewell standing in the yard behind a clump of blue cornflowers with an empty jar in his hand.

"Brodie Lacewell, I swear you don't seem real. The sunshine looks like it's passing right through you. If you just floated away at this very moment, I wouldn't be a bit surprised," she said.

Brodie didn't move.

"Pale blue's your color, Brodie Lacewell. It fits you to a tee. Hey, Brodie!" she shouted. "Soon as you catch that butterfly, go in and see Queen Esther. She's come to stay with us."

Without breaking his staring at the blue flowers, Brodie put a finger to his lips, making the sign of silence.

"If you're still stuck in that spot when I get back, I'm going to shake you, Brodie Lacewell!" called Annie Earle as she moved toward the street, *step-slap, step-slap.*

. . .

The dress got made, and the making of it seemed to put new life into the old Roland household. Annie Earle rushed home from school each day as fast as her lame leg would allow. At times like this it seemed unfair to her that she was the only one in the house who still had to go to school. She was glad to be finishing. She'd never liked it. Never made any real friends. Queen Esther had quit school two years ago. And Brodie Lacewell had never been a day in his life. At least not to regular school. Mama had taught him to read when he was little, and Annie Earle worked on arithmetic with him sometimes. He was quick to learn. The hard part was to keep him from nicktating long enough to do the learning.

Mama spent the week alternating between high excitement and deep sleep. She needed a lot more medication than usual.

When the dress was ready, Brodie Lacewell sewed the pearls around the neckline and on the skirt. They were perfectly spaced, and he didn't drift away from the task, not once.

Queen Esther was everywhere: in the kitchen peeling vegetables, in the parlor dusting, hurrying from the bedroom to the outhouse to empty the night pots. And when there was a lull in the activity, she rubbed Mama's back.

Aunt Charlotte had said Queen Esther had healing hands. Mama remembered. "Aunt Charlotte," she called, "send Queen Esther up to rub my shoulders! They're giving me a fit."

Queen Esther hummed a lulling tune as she rubbed Mama's shoulders. Her delicate fingers were strong and knowing. The ache was soon eased, and Mama dozed again.

Annie Earle watched as Queen Esther rubbed and hummed. Yes, yes, it was the tune, the same tune Queen had hummed years ago when they'd played "sick doll." It all came back to her sharp and clear.

"My doll's got whooping cough," she told Queen. "She's got to stay in her crib all day."

"We get her well," said Queen.

"Yeah, we'll give her a pill. And plenty of apple juice."

"No," said Queen.

"Apple juice will cure her."

"No," said Queen. "I cure her with hands."

"That's silly. How?"

"Like this," said Queen.

She cradled the doll gently and hummed a strange tune, while rubbing the doll's head, face, and chest with her free hand.

Annie Earle reached toward the doll, intending to take it from Queen Esther, but pulled back and listened to the humming. And watched how seriously Queen seemed to go about the curing business with her hands.

"Queen?" she asked cautiously.

But Queen paid no attention. She went on humming and stroking the doll.

Annie Earle tapped Queen on the shoulder and got no response. She was scared. Queen didn't hear her. Queen didn't feel her. She waited nervously until the tune was hummed out.

"There," said Queen, handing Annie Earle the doll. "That baby's all well."

Saturday arrived. The dress was finished. Annie Earle put it on and went to Mama's room to show it off.

"I declare, you're a vision, Annie Earle. You're a vision!" exclaimed Mama.

"Ain't she pretty," added Aunt Charlotte.

"A vision," repeated Mama. "Just be careful how you

get in and out of the buggy tonight. And watch how you sit so as not to crush the skirt. Aunt Charlotte, did you arrange for Mr. Shulken to wait for Annie Earle and bring her home from the dance?"

"Don't you fret, Miss Nel. It's all arranged. Mr. Shulken got a nice buggy, and he be glad to wait for a return fare."

"Can I ride over with Miss Annie Earle and wait in the buggy, then come home with her?" asked Queen Esther.

"That's nice of you, Queen Esther," answered Mama. "But I don't think it's necessary. Mr. Shulken will take good care of Annie Earle."

Queen Esther looked disappointed. She followed Annie Earle to her room.

"Let me rub your feet, Annie Earle, before you put on these satin dancing shoes."

"My feet feel fine," and Annie Earle. "They don't need any rubbing."

"My rubbing keeps off bad things," replied Queen Esther.

"No," said Annie Earle. "I don't believe in that stuff."

"Good luck, then. I wishes you the best of luck, Annie Earle."

"Stop talking like that, Queen Esther. You make me nervous. I don't need your luck."

"Yes, ma'am," replied Queen Esther.

The satin dancing shoes played a new rhythm on the stair treads as Annie Earle went down—*step-click, step-click.*

Aunt Charlotte called from the hallway, "Come on in the kitchen. There's still time to have some fresh-baked pound cake with coffee. You hardly eat a thing all day."

"The smell of that cake does bring my appetite back," replied Annie Earle.

Brodie was already at the table having cake with milk-cut coffee. Queen Esther joined them. Aunt Charlotte sliced thick slabs of cake for everyone and poured a round of coffee.

"You look pretty as Mama tonight," said Brodie.

"She do look pretty in her new dress," said Aunt Charlotte, "but for looks Miss Annie Earle is the spitting image of her daddy. And he was some fine-looking gentleman, I can tell you. From the day Mr. Roland stepped off that logging train, half the petticoats in this town was after him. He could have had his pick. But it was Miss Nel for him right from the start. Annie Earle gets that deep red hair from her daddy."

"Aunt Charlotte, I was six years old when Daddy died. I can remember him very well."

"Me, too," said Brodie. "I was seven."

"Speaking of seven, Lord, it must be close to that time right now," exclaimed Aunt Charlotte. "I told Mr. Shulken to be here with the buggy for Annie Earle by seven sharp. Queen, run see if he be waiting out front."

Queen made a fast sally to the front door and called, "You right, Gramma, the buggy's already here."

Aunt Charlotte quickly brushed Annie Earle's dress for stray cake crumbs. "We be waiting up for you in the parlor," she said.

"No need for that. I'll just slip up to bed when Mr. Shulken brings me back," said Annie Earle.

"We be waiting," replied Queen Esther.

Brodie Lacewell, Aunt Charlotte, and Queen Esther waved from the front porch as Annie Earle settled into the buggy with Mr. Shulken. She glanced back as he drove away. From Mama's upstairs window, a hand with a lace handkerchief moved back and forth.

The Prize

....•——◆——•....

*S*tep-click, step-click. Her footfalls pounded across the porch.

Aunt Charlotte and Queen Esther rushed to the front entrance. Annie Earle was clutching the screen door. Aunt Charlotte!" she wailed. "I could just die!"

"What's wrong?" asked Aunt Charlotte as she gathered Annie Earle in her arms.

"Oh, Aunt Charlotte, I could just die! The most awful thing happened!"

Aunt Charlotte guided her into the parlor, past the sofa where Brodie slept soundly. "Come on and sit down, then tell me."

"I can't sit down!" cried Annie Earle. "I'm bleeding!"

"Sweet Jesus, have mercy!" cried Aunt Charlotte. "Where you hurt, Miss Annie Earle?"

"It's my knee. It happened when I fell."

"How did you fall?" asked Queen Esther.

"Stop asking questions, Queen, and get a basin of water and some of that bird's-eye cotton from the linen closet. Quick! Here, Miss Annie Earle, you just be calm a minute till we get your pretty new dress off."

"It's ripped," cried Annie Earle. "I tore it when I fell. And it's stained down near the hemline."

Aunt Charlotte quickly checked the skirt. A small dark circle surrounded one of the seed pearls.

"Here, honey, it's all right. Just let me slip the dress over your head. Nothing on this skirt, cold water and lemon juice won't soak out."

16

Annie Earle sat on the sofa, pulled up her petticoat, and for the first time looked at her knee. Dried blood was caked around an angry gash and a trail of red droplets dribbled toward the defective foot.

Queen Esther appeared with the water and a soft cotton cloth. "Here, let me mop off this blood and clean up that cut. Water's gonna sting just a little."

Annie Earle sank back into the chair and covered her face with her arm. Queen Esther quickly cleaned the wound and bandaged it with a piece of the soft cotton cloth. She placed the basin with the pinkish water on an end table.

"Let her be," whispered Aunt Charlotte. "Let her be for a minute."

Queen Esther slid back across the rug to Annie Earle and gently removed the satin slippers from her feet. Beginning with a featherlike touch, she massaged Annie Earle's foot. When she first touched the clubfoot, Annie Earle gave a convulsive twitch and pulled it from Queen's hands. But Queen Esther continued the stroking movements in the air, just above the defective foot, then gradually moved closer and closer until she was gently rubbing the foot again. This time Annie Earle didn't pull away. Queen Esther hummed a strange tune that fitted the rhythm of the rubbing. Gradually Annie Earle lowered her arm, exposing a flushed and tear-streaked face. Queen stopped humming. The room was completely silent.

"Run, Sister Annie Earle, run! It's got claws!"

Everyone jumped at the outcry. The sound came from across the room. Brodie Lacewell was sitting up on the sofa, eyes staring straight ahead, trancelike. He stood up and walked toward the three women.

"Hide!" he shouted. "Get inside the house! It's got big claws, Annie Earle!"

Aunt Charlotte quickly crossed to Brodie and slapped him sharply on the cheek. "Brodie! Brodie Lacewell! Wake up. Come out of it. Shake that mare!" she cried.

Brodie shook his head, fluttered his eyes and rubbed them with his fists. He made a whimpering sound and then focused on Aunt Charlotte. "It was terrible," he said. "A big orange-and-black bird was about to snatch Annie Earle. He almost got her."

"You was just dreaming," said Aunt Charlotte soothingly. "It was one of your bad mares, Brodie Lacewell. You was walking around again, too."

"Go to bed, Brodie," said Annie Earle. "I'm all right."

Obediently Brodie walked toward the hall. He paused and turned back when he reached the doorway. "You look different, Annie Earle. You sure that terrible bird didn't catch you?"

"It was one of your mares, Brodie. Go to bed now," replied Annie Earle.

Brodie Lacewell left the room. Aunt Charlotte walked to the door and looked down the hallway.

"Thank the Lord, he come out of it without having a seizure. It's a wonder Miss Nel ain't waked up with all this racket. But I ain't heard her bell. She must be sleeping mighty deep."

Aunt Charlotte returned to Annie Earle. "Honey, you want to tell Aunt Charlotte what happened? How'd you fall, child?"

"There was a door prize. Everybody got a ticket when they came in. After the third dance they had a drawing up on the platform. And my number won. I couldn't believe it. Mr. Oldham kept calling, 'Will number forty-seven please come to the platform? The winner is number forty-seven. I just kept looking at my number and it was forty-seven plain as day. But I couldn't move. Finally Mr.

Oldham said, 'Last call for number forty-seven. Does anybody have number forty-seven? If no one comes forward, I must draw another number.'"

"How come you didn't call out?" asked Queen Esther.

"I did. Finally I did," said Annie Earle. "I called out, 'Wait! I've got the winning number.' I was so excited. I'd been standing around doing nothing all night. Just watching everybody else dance. I think that fast Tommy Hickman from my class danced with every girl there but me. Now it was my turn to do something. I hurried to the platform. Mr. Oldham was saying, 'We have a winner. A winner! And it looks like Miss Annie Earle Roland.' It seemed like hundreds of people were in the way. I had to push through the whole crowd. When I got to the platform, my heart was pounding and my cheeks were burning up. There weren't any handrails on the steps to the platform. But I was so pleased I just said to myself, 'Annie Earle, you don't need any handrails to get yourself up to that platform. You're a winner, Annie Earle. And a winner can manage four little old steps.'

"Aunt Charlotte, I made three steps with nothing to hold on to. And I thought I had made the last one when my dress caught under my bad foot and I fell flat on my face."

Annie Earle pushed from the chair and step-slapped over to the fireplace, where she stood with her back to Aunt Charlotte and Queen.

"Poor child, poor child," chanted Aunt Charlotte. Then Annie Earle heard her whisper to Queen Esther, "The Roland luck dogs all this family. Sometimes I think this child is different, but that same luck dogs her, too. Dogs her without relief."

"I knowed I should have rubbed her feet. I knowed it," muttered Queen Esther.

Annie Earle turned to face them. "It wasn't just the falling," she said. "I'm used to falling, though I wish I could be invisible when it happens with people looking on. Here I was, a winner. First time I ever won anything in my whole life. Climbing up on that platform with everybody clapping. Every eye in the dance hall on me. I was so ashamed. 'Get home, Annie Earle, get home' was all I could think."

Aunt Charlotte smiled and pushed strands of deep red hair from Annie Earle's forehead. "They's nothing to be ashamed of, child. Fact is, today is a big occasion. You got yourself out of this house and went out to that dance like a grown-up woman. You is a woman now, Annie Earle. Ain't that something—my baby's a woman!"

"I don't want to be a woman. I just want to be Annie Earle."

"You still going to be Annie Earle. You be a woman, too. And that means Miss Annie Earle with a lot more power. You'll see, you'll see," Aunt Charlotte said.

"Did you get the prize?" asked Queen Esther.

"Oh, the prize. Mr. Oldham helped me up and handed me the prize. I don't know if I thanked him or not. 'Get out of here, Annie Earle,' I was saying to myself. 'Get out of sight of all these people. If you can just make it to the buggy.' That nice dark buggy, carrying me home. Maybe Mama was right. Maybe I *should* stay home."

"You *did* get the prize!" cried Queen.

"It's on the front porch. I left it on the rocker on the porch."

Queen Esther darted out of the room. In a moment she returned with a small box wrapped in pink marbleized paper and tied with lavender ribbon bows.

"Come on, Annie Earle, open the box!" cried Queen Esther. "We all dying to see."

With some help with the bows from Queen, Annie Earle carefully peeled away the wrappings. She lifted the lid and peered into the mass of crushed snowy tissue. A small porcelain arm reached through the paper. Annie Earle lifted the object from the tissue. The raised arm belonged to a dancer poised on one foot atop a music box.

"You had to win that prize!" exclaimed Queen Esther. "You had to, 'cause you're gonna dance just like this doll."

Aunt Charlotte and Annie Earle stared at Queen with puzzled looks on their faces.

"And the dress. The dress on the dancer is the same color as your dancing dress. Royal blue."

Annie Earle laughed. "You're too much, Queen Esther. Let me wind up this royal blue dancing girl and see if she's saved a dance for me."

Around and around the tiny figure turned to a lively, tinkling tune.

"Let's dance, Annie Earle, let's dance," said Queen Esther as she swayed to the rhythm of the music box.

Annie Earle looked doubtful.

"You be fine with the bandage on," Queen Esther told her.

Annie Earle moved as commanded.

"Raise one arm," sang Queen Esther to the music box tune. "Balance on your strong good foot," she continued. "Lift your bad foot under your skirt like the dancing doll. Now give me your other hand."

Annie Earle looked apprehensive, but she carried out the commands. Queen Esther, holding Annie Earle's hand, began to parade her in a circle in time to the music, just like the dancer on the music box. Gradually Annie Earle began to smile, and Queen Esther added a few funny, shimmylike movements to her walk as she paraded around. They finished several circles before the music box wound down, and the tinkling sounds ground to a halt.

Queen Esther let go of Annie Earle's hand and sat down on the rug.

"I'm drunk!" exclaimed Annie Earle as she staggered toward the sofa and collapsed in a fit of giggles.

Queen Esther joined in the giggles. Aunt Charlotte beamed at the two girls and breathed a deep sigh of relief.

Annie Earle recovered abruptly from her giggles. "Mama," she said. "I got to show Mama my prize."

"She be sleeping now," Aunt Charlotte reminded her.

"Let's tiptoe up to her room and put my prize on the table next to her bed, so she'll see it first thing in the morning," said Annie Earle.

"I think she like that," said Aunt Charlotte.

The procession moved slowly up the stairs. Annie Earle was especially careful not to thump too loudly for fear of waking Mama. About halfway up the stairs she looked back and saw that Queen Esther was not following. "Aren't you coming, Queen Esther?" she whispered.

Queen Esther hesitated for a moment, then shook her head.

Aunt Charlotte and Annie Earle moved quietly and slowly upward. When they reached Mama's room, Aunt Charlotte gently opened the door, allowing a swatch of light to cut into the room from the gas jet in the hallway. A patch of moonlight washed through the window, cutting a jagged pattern across Mama's chaise longue. One of Mama's arms was highlighted in the moonbeams. It was hanging limply toward the floor with loose fingers that seemed to be pointing to the overturned bottle and the scattered pills that dotted the cabbage-rose-patterned carpet. Mama's face was in darkness.

Aunt Charlotte quickly crossed the room to the chaise longue. In one movement she dropped to her knees and lifted the limp arm. Her fingers felt for a pulse.

"Aunt Charlotte, Mama!" cried Annie Earle. "Is Mama all right? Something's wrong with Mama. Is she dead?"

"No, child, your mama's not dead," answered Aunt Charlotte. "But she's sick bad. Call Queen Esther. We got to send for Dr. Whittaker."

"But what's wrong with Mama?"

"Hurry, child. Call Queen. We need the doctor fast."

Aunt Charlotte scooped up the pills, replaced them in the bottle, and then lighted the lamp on Mama's night table. She turned up the wick to brighten the light, revealing the dreadful beauty of Mama's pale and ravaged face.

As Annie Earle thumped heavily from the room she heard Aunt Charlotte whisper, "Miss Nel, Miss Nel, I was so hoping you would hold on for a little longer."

Aunt Kat and Uncle Major

Aunt Charlotte got her wish: Mama held on. Dr. Whittaker said it was a blessing Annie Earle had decided to go up to Mama's room. She barely squeezed through this time. If they had found her the next morning, it would have been too late. The stomach pump wouldn't have done the job. "Yes, sir," he said, "Miss Penelope is a very lucky lady."

Aunt Charlotte and Annie Earle looked at the pale, fragile figure they had spent so many years caring for. Aunt Charlotte shook her head and replied, "No, Doctor, there ain't no luck for Miss Nel. Leastwise no good luck."

"Well, I know she's in good care with you, Charlotte. I want you to keep her medicine downstairs in the kitchen. Bring up one dose at a time with her meals. We don't want Miss Penelope making a mistake about her dosage, now, do we? That's what it was, you know, a mistake. She got mixed up on her dosage. It'll be better if we let Aunt Charlotte take care of that. You understand, Annie Earle?"

"Yes, Dr. Whittaker, I understand. Thank you for explaining to us what happened. That's what we'll tell anybody who inquires about Mama."

"Charlotte, in Miss Penelope's condition I think you ought to send for Katherine. It wouldn't be right not to notify her sister."

"Dr. Whittaker, you know Mama and Aunt Kat don't see eye to eye," said Annie Earle.

"I realize that, but Katherine is her nearest of kin and she ought to know."

"We'll send word in the morning by Queen Esther," answered Aunt Charlotte.

Dr. Whittaker left the room and started down the stairs. Annie Earle followed him to the foot of the stairs and stood there gripping the finial on the newel post. Queen Esther sat on the edge of a chair nearby, alert and uneasy.

"Your mama is all right now," Dr. Whittaker told Annie Earle. "She'll probably sleep most of tomorrow, so don't go bothering her. I'll be back in the afternoon to check on her. Why don't you all get to bed now. That's where I'm headed."

A hundred questions were lurking in Annie Earle's mind, but none of them could find a way out. She just bobbed her head as Dr. Whittaker lumbered by wearily. Suddenly she was aware of the dull ache in her foot and leg. She felt as leaden and tired as the old doctor who had just pulled Mama through.

"Queen Esther," asked Annie Earle, "would you sleep in my room tonight?"

Queen Esther nodded and followed Annie Earle up the stairs.

At breakfast Aunt Charlotte spoke about sending word to Miss Katherine. "Dr. Whittaker advised us to send for Miss Kat," she said as casually as she could put it.

"Mama can't stand Aunt Kat, even when she's well," said Annie Earle. "Why do we have to send for her? I don't like Aunt Kat, either."

"Aunt Kat scares me," said Brodie Lacewell.

"Now, listen, Miss Kat's your closest relation. You both ought to try to be friendly with her," said Aunt Charlotte.

"I'd just as soon try making friends with a rattlesnake!" declared Annie Earle.

"Now, I promised Dr. Whittaker we'd send word," said Aunt Charlotte. "That much I got to do. Maybe she won't come. Maybe she'll just send word back to let her know if we need anything."

"She'll come," predicted Annie Earle.

"Now, listen carefully, Queen Esther," said Aunt Charlotte. "I want you to go over to Miss Kat's house and say Miss Nel had a bad spell last night. We had to have Dr. Whittaker and he felt Miss Kat ought to know. You can tell her Miss Nel be resting now, and the doctor don't want her bothered for a while. Just tell her that. And don't answer any questions if she picks you. Just be polite and say you don't know."

"You want me to play the dumb pickaninny if Miss Kat picks me?" asked Queen Esther. "Yas'um, Miss Kat, Miss Nel be sick bad. No, ma'am, Miss Kat, I don't know how come she sick bad. I'se woolly-headed and mighty sleepy when the doctor come. I don't rightly remember what all happened. I'se scared of sick folks. I ain't been near Miss Nel's room. All I know is what Gramma Charlotte told me to say. I got to be hightailing it back before I gets a licking from my gramma."

Queen Esther's performance set everyone at the kitchen table laughing. Even Brodie Lacewell. Annie Earle exclaimed, "Queen Esther, you're just what Aunt Kat deserves!"

Aunt Charlotte stopped laughing abruptly. "I don't like no granddaughter of mine playing dumb nigger. Just give Miss Kat the message the way I told you and come on back."

Queen Esther left the house after the breakfast things

were cleared away. Annie Earle thumped her way to the front porch and plopped down in her thinking rocker. Brodie Lacewell followed and settled himself on the porch steps. He cupped his chin in one hand and got set for a deep spell of nicktating. For once Annie Earle made no attempt to break it up. She began pushing the chair with her strong foot back and forth. She was thinking what would happen if Mama died. She'd thought of it before but always pushed it aside. Last night it had loomed up urgent, dark, and frightening. Now, for the first time, she faced it.

Only poor, sickly Mama keeps us together as a family. Annie Earle, you could hold this family together if they'd let you. But they won't. You're too young and lame, they'll say. They'll separate us sure as life if Mama goes. They'll send poor Brodie off to some home where there's strangers and bars on the windows. Brodie'll just die in a place like that. Brodie needs sunlight and flowers and butterflies and people he knows. I wish I could work magic. I'd change Aunt Charlotte to white and make her my blood kin, and we'd live here happy all our days, and Queen Esther and I would be real sisters, and nobody could touch us ever.

Annie Earle's strong foot plunged against the floor, rocking the chair furiously. She closed her eyes and gripped the chair arms tightly, blotting out her fantasies.

Suddenly she halted the rocking, stood up, and hissed, "Damn, damn, damn!" She looked at Brodie Lacewell, shimmering in the morning sun, lost in deep nicktation, and yelled, "Brodie! Brodie Lacewell! Snap out of it! You just can't sit there nicktating! The world's falling apart!"

At the sound, a flurry of tiny yellow butterflies fled from the sweetshrub bush growing near the steps. They circled Brodie's head and scattered toward the portulaca beds. Brodie remained as still and as translucent as an alabaster statue.

Aunt Kat sent word by Queen Esther that she'd be around at twelve o'clock sharp. That way Uncle Major could join her on his Sunday dinner break from the railway station. The Atlantic Coast Line was a strict company and Uncle Major was proud of his long record as stationmaster-for-freight. Aunt Kat was strict about everything, especially money and the upbringing of children. She never failed to declare her special talents for handling both. Uncle Major spent a lot of time bobbing his head in agreement with Aunt Kat and glancing at his big gold watch, a convenient reminder that he must soon be off to keep important schedules.

Annie Earle and Queen Esther watched from the porch as the two dark-clad figures invaded the front yard. From somber bonnet to pointed, pinched shoes, Aunt Kat was in deepest mourning. She prided herself on having worn one shade or another of mourning since her mother put her in a black dress at the age of nine to attend her grandmother's funeral. Black serge was Uncle Major's uniform since he had joined the Atlantic Coast Line as a teenage sweep-boy. They swooped down the walk like two big crows, in sharp contrast to the dazzling array of bright flowers that bordered the path.

"Don't they look like funeral parlor directors sniffing out business?" whispered Annie Earle.

"More like bad-luck birds of prey," answered Queen Esther.

"Morning, Annie Earle," snapped Aunt Kat. "What's going on here? I've never heard such a garbled message as that colored girl came bringing this morning. You sure she's right in the head? I couldn't get a straight line out of her. The more I questioned her the worse she got. I do believe she's half-witted."

"Aunt Kat, this is Queen Esther, Aunt Charlotte's granddaughter. You've seen her before," answered Annie Earle.

"Charlotte's got so many granddaughters, I can't keep them straight. But I didn't come here to get Charlotte's family tree straightened out. God knows, that would take some unraveling. What's the matter with Nel?"

"Mama had a bad spell last night. Dr. Whittaker said we almost lost her," replied Annie Earle.

"Let me see Nel. I've been through spells with her long before you were born. She can't fool me. I know all her tricks. I've seen her pull spells just to keep from facing up. Let me see Nel. Nobody knows her like me."

Uncle Major pulled out his big gold watch and cleared his throat.

"We can't spend our whole dinner hour standing here on the front porch. Mr. Major has to be back at the ACL freight office by one o'clock sharp," she added.

Aunt Charlotte appeared at the front door.

"Good morning, Miss Kat. It's mighty good of you to drop by. Miss Nel had a bad spell last night. But she be sleeping now. She don't need to be disturbed. Dr. Whittaker give her something to make her rest. She'll be all right soon as she sleeps some more."

"I intend to see my sister," said Aunt Kat as she pushed past Aunt Charlotte and headed toward the stairs. Uncle Major trailed behind. The staircase bore the weight of a procession. Aunt Charlotte, Annie Earle, and Queen Esther followed.

Aunt Kat and Uncle Major barged into Mama's room. Aunt Charlotte held up a restraining arm and kept the others in the hall outside the slightly ajar door.

"Nel, Nel," called Aunt Kat, "can you hear me? Wake up, Nel. I want to talk to you. It's me, Kat, your sister. Mr. Major's here. We've come to help you, Nel."

"Kat? What are you doing here, Kat?" The little group in the hall could barely catch the soft, weak words coming from Mama.

"Nel, you look terrible," said Aunt Kat. "I just don't see how things can go on like this. I don't see that you're capable of running the affairs of your family. Now, Nel, we've talked about this before. And it looks like the time has come when it can't be put off. You're in bad shape, Nel. As your closest kin, I think the time has come to grant me power of attorney. Somebody's got to take care of your affairs. Nel, are you listening to me?"

"Kat, Big Kat," Mama whispered. "Sister Kat, I'm listening. And you scare me, chill to the bone you scare me. I'm just hanging here by a thread, Kat. But it's a thread that isn't broken yet. I almost snapped it last night, but it's mended today, and I'm hanging on."

"Nel, you're not fit to be bringing up a daughter with an affliction and a son that's feebleminded. Institutions are what you need. Both those children need to be in a good religious institution. You are simply not equipped to deal with them, Nel. They're growing up with a bunch of niggers in charge. God will never forgive you, Nel. Think how God must feel about your situation. Nel, it's the eleventh hour. Mr. Major and I are here, ready and willing to take over."

"Kat, leave my room," said Mama, with a slow deliberate space between each word. "Leave my house. And get out of my life and my children's lives. You've just given me the strength to hold on. Thank you for that, Kat. Thank you for coming, Kat. I might have defaulted to you and Mr. Major. You better go now, Kat. I need to rest."

"Nel, you're out of your mind. You're ungrateful and you're not responsible. Don't push me, Nel. I may just have to go to court and have you declared—"

"Beg pardon, Miss Kat," called Aunt Charlotte as she entered the room, "but Dr. Whittaker said Miss Nel should rest and not talk too much. I'm afraid she's about to overdo it."

Aunt Kat and Uncle Major stomped out of the room. As they passed Annie Earle, Aunt Kat hissed under her breath to Uncle Major, "Such uppity niggers. I wouldn't stand for them in my house one minute."

Halfway down the stairs, Aunt Kat paused, looked up at Annie Earle, and said, "There's no responsible person in this house."

Annie Earle replied, "I'm responsible, Aunt Kat."

"You're just a child, Annie Earle, a poor, afflicted child."

"I'm responsible and I'm a woman now, Aunt Kat," said Annie Earle calmly.

"Nonsense!" shouted Aunt Kat. "Come along, Mr. Major. You mustn't be late. The Atlantic Coast Line is never late."

Uncle Major looked at his watch again. Aunt Kat turned to face Annie Earle. "You'll be hearing from me real soon," she said, with a twisted little smile that looked even more threatening than her words sounded.

The dark pair left the cool house and headed into the blazing sunshine. Annie Earle shaded her eyes and watched them as they receded down the front walk.

From the protective shelter of a flame azalea bush, she heard Brodie Lacewell say, "Annie Earle, Annie Earle, the big dark bird with the sharp claws is gone."

The Vulture

···•───◆──◆───•···

For Brodie it was easy. The fear of the big bird with the sharp claws vanished when Aunt Kat closed the garden gate on his private little world. But rock as hard as she could, Annie Earle could not rid herself of the dark presence hovering over her, ready to pounce. She was afraid for Brodie, for Aunt Charlotte, for herself and Mama. Strangely, she felt no fear for Queen Esther. She pumped the rocking chair briskly, thinking of Queen.

Queen's different. She's never been a house cat. Not Queen. Too wild and free and close to magic. Tame cats lose their mysteries. Queen's never let go of them. She's the only one of us that Aunt Kat can't touch. Sometimes I think Queen can look right through me, can even hear all the unspoken things I never said.

At night the dark shadows of frightening legal terminology invaded her dreams. In Aunt Kat's voice she heard the words *power of attorney, legal guardian, court order, writ, determination of insanity* flitting around the edges of sleep, lurking in her bedroom from sundown to sunrise. Each morning she woke with fear clutching her heart until she checked Mama's room and found the slender breath of life still holding. That cold night-scare saddled her like a chronic ailment, easing up by day, but always returning with nightfall. It was a comfort to have Queen in the house. She was glad Mama had agreed to keep her on.

They were snapping green string beans in the privacy of the backyard gazebo.

"You acting these days like somebody put a spell on you," said Queen Esther.

Annie Earle stared into the intricate latticework of the gazebo and made no answer, a half-snapped string bean clutched in her hand.

"You keep drifting off like that, folks gone soon say you acting like Brodie with his nicktating. You listening to me, Annie Earle?"

"I hear you, Queen. I hear you plain as day. And maybe you're right. Maybe somebody has put a spell on me. I feel trapped. It's funny how people you love who're as weak and frail as Brodie and Mama can trap you as tight as somebody you really hate, like Aunt Kat. I've been having troubling dreams lately."

"I know what be troubling your dreams," said Queen softly. "Miss Kat's enough to trouble the devil hisself."

"I wouldn't say this to a soul except you, Queen. The only way I can think of Aunt Kat is like some big, hungry vulture circling around our house. And every circle she makes she comes a little closer. Each circle gets tighter and tighter. She's waiting for Mama to make a move, get worse, or maybe even die."

"Hush!" commanded Queen Esther. "Don't say that word. Saying it means accepting it." She leaned close to Annie Earle and whispered in her ear, "There be ways to put Miss Kat in her place, you know."

Annie Earle's hand released the bruised string bean she had been squeezing between her fingers.

"What kind of ways?" she asked softly.

"Like I said, you acting like they's some kind of spell on you. There be ways to shift a spell off you and put it on somebody else, if that's what you want."

"You know I don't believe in that root-working mess."

"Maybe you never needed to believe before."

"What are you getting at, Queen?"

"I be friends with Granny Buzzard, the best conjure woman in the root-working business."

Annie Earle laughed.

"You making fun of Granny Buzzard?"

"No, I'm not funning about Granny Buzzard. But it did strike me funny that I called Aunt Kat a vulture and right away you suggested Granny Buzzard as the way to get her off our backs. Fight a vulture with a buzzard. Two birds of a kind. Don't you think that's funny?"

"No," said Queen. "I never seen nothing funny about Granny Buzzard. I seen her spells work. She scares the bejesus out of me, but I be drawn to her. She laid her hand on me when I was just a little girl and said I had the calling. I don't know what that means, far as I'm concerned. But I don't doubt for a minute that old woman got strong power."

"Oh, Queen, I wish it was as easy as that. We'd take a little money to Granny Buzzard, she'd put some roots together in a conjure spell, and Aunt Kat would leave us in peace. The Buzzard outwits the Vulture. Lord, wouldn't that be great!"

"You got five dollars you can lay your hand on without letting anybody know?"

"I fear root working is a pretty weak defense against legal action. Mama got notice this week from Powell and Powell, attorneys-at-law, that their client Aunt Kat was filing a petition to become legal guardian of Mama and me and Brodie. Aunt Kat tells everybody all over town that she's only thinking of our good, doing what any Christian woman would do. Aunt Kat doesn't give a damn about us. It's Mama's property and money she's after."

"Lord, that vulture is coming in to roost. You better think on what I told you."

"You girls got them string beans shelled?" called Aunt Charlotte from the back porch.

"Just about!" shouted Queen Esther. "Now, don't you say a word to Gramma Charlotte or anybody else about Granny Buzzard," cautioned Queen. "But you think on it."

Although she was not ready to admit it to Queen Esther, Annie Earle was already thinking on the subject. Her fingers rapidly snapped the remaining string beans in her basin. "Let's get these beans in to Aunt Charlotte before she calls again."

As the two girls reached the kitchen, they could hear the front doorbell ringing.

"Queen Esther, see who be at the front door," said Aunt Charlotte. "My hands is covered with flour dough."

Queen darted down the hallway as the bell rang with repeated insistency. She flipped the night latch and opened the door. Aunt Kat exploded into the hall.

"Deaf or dead, I never know which when I come to this house," she snapped. "I've been ringing that bell long enough to alert the whole neighborhood. I've come to check on my sister. I trust even she is up by this belated hour."

Without waiting for Queen's reply, Aunt Kat headed up the stairs. Queen dashed back to the kitchen.

"It's Miss Kat, and she's on the way up to Miss Nel's room!"

"Just what Mama needs to give her a real setback," said Annie Earle. "I'm going up."

"Listen a minute, Annie Earle," said Aunt Charlotte. "Be careful what you say to Miss Kat. She be dangerous. Hold your tongue. I'll wait a few minutes, then come up and say Miss Nel has to take her medicine. That way maybe we can keep Miss Kat from staying too long."

Annie Earle pulled herself up the stairs, thinking, *I'll have to bite my tongue to hold it with Aunt Kat.*

To her surprise she found the sisters quietly exchanging almost formal greetings. She stood listening at the doorway.

"I'm happy to see you looking so much better," said Aunt Kat.

"It's real nice of you to worry about me, Sister Kat."

"You do realize that I'm acting out of concern for you and your children?"

"Yes, Kat, your concern is real touching."

"Well, I thought I should come over myself as soon as those papers from Powell and Powell had arrived. We're family, Nel, and legal documents can appear so cold. I just want to reassure you that all those high-flown lawyer terms are just there because it's necessary to keep things legal. But don't forget, I'm your only sister, Nel, and I do intend to temper legality with compassion. It's going to work out just fine. And it's going to take a big load off your frail back. It's the least Mr. Major and I can do."

"You're putting yourself out too much as it is. I never want to impose on people, you know. Not even if they're family."

"It's my Christian duty, Nel. You don't know how happy it makes me that you see it my way. I tell you the truth. I really expected to have to fight you on this one. Now, if you'll just sign those papers and send them back to Mr. Powell, you won't have a thing to worry about."

"I'll be taking care of those papers later today. I'm

sorry if I've seemed fractious and stubborn toward you, Sister Kat. My ailments make me act like that sometimes. I need to rest now, so I'll say good day to you, Kat."

"And a good day to you, Nel. You'll see. I'll have things straightened out around here before you know it."

Annie Earle ducked quickly behind the large linen press that stood in the hall just outside Mama's bedroom. Aunt Kat moved down the stairs like a dark shadow. When the front door closed with a click, Annie Earle hurried into Mama's room.

"Mama!" she cried. "I just heard you and Aunt Kat talking. I can't believe what you said!"

"Child, come over here. Come sit on the chaise with me."

Annie Earle step-slapped to her mother and sat nervously on the edge of the chaise.

"You didn't listen carefully, Annie Earle. And, thank God, neither did Sister Kat. All I told her was that I'd be taking care of the notice sent me by the Powell lawyers. And that I intend to do."

"But, Mama, it sounded to me like that's just the thing to give Aunt Kat control over all of us."

"When you're sick as long as I've been, you have plenty of time to think. Most of the time it's bad thinking, just dwelling on your ailments. But sometimes a sickness can make your thinking sharp—not all the time, just sometimes, like a sharp, clear ray of sunlight finding a crack in the darkest cloud storm. I think I've found a hole in the black clouds."

"Oh, Mama, I don't know what you're talking about."

"Listen, Annie Earle, you've got to do an errand for me. I've written a note to Mr. Sears at the bank. I want you to take it to him before the bank closes at three o'clock today."

"Mama, please tell me what you're planning."

"I'm plotting a way around Sister Kat. And I'm making myself be nice to her till we're safely by. That's all you need to know, baby. There's the note over there on my dresser. Now I really am going to take me a nap."

Annie Earle wanted desperately to know what Mama had written in the note to Mr. Sears. She knew it would be useless to try to get more information out of Mama. She worried.

What if Mama has written a bunch of nonsense to Mr. Sears. It will only help Aunt Kat make her case. Maybe I should steam the envelope open and see for sure what Mama is up to. No, I can't do that to poor Mama. She's trusting me to do something that she thinks is really important. I'll have to do it. But I sure need some insurance to fall back on.

Queen Esther was standing in the hall when Annie Earle reached the bottom of the stairs.

"Big bird of prey checking out her hunting ground," said Queen.

"I feel so helpless and mad at the same time!" snapped Annie Earle. "I wish to God I could click my fingers and be three years older, legal age. I'd know how to deal with Aunt Kat. With you and Aunt Charlotte, we don't need anybody to look after us. Three years seems like a lifetime away. Oh, Queen, how are we going to hold Aunt Kat off that long?"

Tears of frustration dribbled onto Annie Earle's cheeks.

Instead of answering her question, Queen Esther sang a little ditty.

> *"Oh, the Buzzard caught the Vulture,*
> *What a dirty shame!*
> *The Buzzard whipped the Vulture,*
> *At the Vulture's own game!"*

"I'm thinking about it," said Annie Earle. "I'm going on an errand to the bank. I'll let you know when I get back."

As she walked to the bank, Annie Earle had thoughts of Granny Buzzard's magic pouncing around in her head like a persistent cat worrying a half-dead mouse. She'd kill off the idea, and half a block later it would roll over and show signs of life again. She'd toy with it and consider. *What's to be lost? Five dollars, maybe. What's to be gained? If Queen could be believed? It's all a bunch of mumbo jumbo for colored folks who don't know any better.* Pow! She killed it for good.

At the bank she was immediately sent into Mr. Sears's private office. Mrs. Penelope Roland maintained one of the largest accounts with the Vineland Savings Company.

"Well, this is a nice surprise and a pleasure for me. How's Miss Annie Earle today?" asked Mr. Sears.

"Fine, sir," she answered.

"Your mother's doing as well as can be expected, I trust," said Mr. Sears.

"Mama's all right, thank you, sir."

"Well, what can I do for you?"

"I have a note from my mother." Annie Earle thrust the envelope forward.

Mr. Sears took the envelope and placed it on his desk.

"Aren't you going to open it?" asked Annie Earle. "I'll wait to see if you want to send Mama a reply."

"Oh, yes. I'll just take a look at it," said Mr. Sears, reaching for his glasses with one hand and for the letter with the other. He carefully slit the envelope with a silver opener that had a coiled snake for a handle. Quickly he read the two pages of writing on the lavender paper. "Yes. I see what you mean," he mumbled. "There is a reply. Tell Miss Penelope I'll be over on my way home, around five-thirty this afternoon."

"Thank you, sir," said Annie Earle. "I'll tell her to expect you at five-thirty." She felt relieved that Mama's note made sense to Mr. Sears.

On the return trip the Granny Buzzard mouse took on new life. Annie Earle's head was swimming with ideas. Everybody around her was making moves—Aunt Kat, Mama, Mr. Sears, the Powell attorneys-at-law. She was the only one standing still and having nightmares.

"Queen Esther! Queen, where are you?" she called from the backyard. Queen poked her head out of the kitchen door, holding a wet dishrag in her hand.

"I'm right here, elbow deep in dishes," she answered. "Is something wrong?"

"Just about everything," answered Annie Earle. "I've been known to accuse Brodie of nicktating while the world falls apart around him, but I'm just as bad. Brodie does it because nicktating is what comes naturally to him. But being scared to make a move is something I've lived with long enough."

"You some stirred up. But what you mean?"

"I mean get rid of that wet dishrag and be ready to go with me to Granny Buzzard's in five minutes. I've got to give a message to Mama and scare up five dollars, and we're off."

Annie Earle left Queen stunned by her announcement and plodded off to Mama's room to deliver Mr. Sears's message.

Message delivered and five dollars stuffed into her pocket, she came down the stairs. "Queen Esther!" she called. "Where are you?"

"She say tell you she be in the gazebo," answered Aunt Charlotte.

In the gazebo she found Queen looking troubled. "What's the matter?" she asked. "It was your idea. Let's get on over to Granny Buzzard's before I change my mind."

"Can't go now," said Queen.

"Why not?"

"Wrong time."

"Queen, you drive me to distraction sometimes. You sat right here shelling string beans just a couple of hours ago, telling me Granny Buzzard was the answer to our troubles. Has she lost her power since this morning?"

"No, Granny Buzzard ain't lost no power. Arrangements has to be made. And broad daylight, with God-knows-who seeing you go to Granny's house, just ain't the time for this business. We'll go after dark."

"Well, I'm hopped up to do it right now. I just hope my mind holds steady on it till nightfall."

"There's something else, too," said Queen.

"Has Granny's price gone up?" asked Annie Earle.

"No," said Queen. "But we got to make it look like two colored girls going to visit Granny, just in case somebody spot us coming or going."

"Well, I might have a hard time passing," said Annie Earle.

"I make arrangements and figure it out by time it be dark," said Queen Esther. "You just work on holding firm in your mind."

The Buzzard

A nnie Earle waited until Aunt Charlotte had made her final trek up the stairs with Mama's bedtime medicine and then gone off to bed. She checked to make sure Brodie was in his room tinkering with his butterfly collection.

Annie Earle and Queen Esther slipped cautiously out of the back door. It was a dark, starless, murky-moon night, just the kind Queen would have ordered if she could have had her pick. The two figures walked slowly through the edge of Haiti, the name the colored folks had given to their part of town years ago. They spelled it like the Republic of Haiti, but they called it "Haytie." One of the figures was clothed in a long black dress, black gloves, and a wide-brimmed black hat, with dark mourning veils cascading around the brim, concealing the face. The other woman seemed to be supporting and consoling the black-clad figure.

"I can't help it but I feel foolish in Mama's old mourning clothes," said Annie Earle.

"Well, it's the only way I could think to get you to Granny Buzzard and back without half the town knowing what be going on. It would be some kind of news if word got out Granny Buzzard be working roots for white folks. You walk into her house with everybody looking and knowing who you was, I doubts Granny would take your case."

"Doubts is just what I'm having again," said Annie Earle. "I'm teetering on turning back."

"You going for royal blue? Or you gonna switch back to that pale, washed-out blue?" asked Queen Esther.

"Speaking in riddles seems to be the only way you can talk these days," said Annie Earle.

"You well know what I mean," replied Queen.

"I know. How much farther to Granny Buzzard's?"

"It be the last house on the edge of Haiti, set off by itself. It be near about smothered in cedar trees. Granny the only one not scared to grow cedar trees in her yard. You usually see cedar trees just in cemeteries. Everybody but Granny Buzzard says they's bad luck. If you plant a cedar in your yard, you die when the cedar get big enough to shadow your grave. That's what they say."

They walked on in silence. A yard dog barked, causing Annie Earle to jump and stumble. Queen Esther caught her arm and steadied her. "We's near about there," she said. "That old yard hound be tied up at the last house before Granny Buzzard's."

Soon Queen was leading Annie Earle through what felt in the dark like a tunnel of low-branching trees. A pungent cedar smell perfumed the air. The path was so narrow they had to go single file. Annie Earle held one hand in front of her face to guard against the scratchy slap of the dense cedar branches. With the other hand she held onto Queen's shoulder to guide her through the darkness.

"You were right. I feel like I'm about to smother in these cedar trees."

They popped through the last of the dense branches and stood before the strangest house Annie Earle had ever seen. In the murky moonlight she could see it was made of logs, boards, rusty sheets of tin roofing, shipping crates, and odd bits and pieces of wood and metal. It looked like someone had taken a junk pile and shaped it into a cabin. A dim light flickered behind a frayed length of flower-printed cloth that hung in the doorway. Wisps of white smoke drifted out of a crooked chimney that leaned against the house. Annie Earle wondered if it was safe to enter a house that looked as if it might collapse if one so much as sneezed in it. But Queen Esther was already rapping against the doorjamb with a stick.

"Door's open. You don't have to bang!" called a raspy voice from within.

Annie Earle took a step back, but Queen Esther lifted the cloth in the doorway and held it to one side, motioning her to enter first. With a thumping heart, Annie Earle stepped through the doorway and into a room that was even more surprising than the outside of the strange house.

The walls and entire ceiling of the room were completely covered with bits and pieces of colored papers—fancy wrapping paper, fragments of old posters advertising the county fair and the Cole Brothers Circus and vaudeville shows that had stopped in the town for a single night. Postcards and bright labels from canned goods, soap and candy wrappings filled in the spaces between the larger papers and posters. Silver chewing-gum wrappers flickered like stars on the ceiling, reflecting the sputtering light from the candles stuffed in dark blue milk of magnesia bottles. Annie Earle felt surrounded by a crazy quilt of many colors.

The smell of the cabin was as powerful as the multicolored walls. Sassafrass, rabbit tobacco, Saint John's weed, catnip, wormwood, spearmint, and dried mullein hanging in bunches from the ceiling made a heady mix of odors. Fumes from a steaming pot in the smoldering fireplace pierced through the dried herb odor with a sharp, spicy clove, cinnamon, and vinegar smell. A sweet, mellow tobacco scent circled lazily on the smoke cloud coming from Granny Buzzard's pipe.

Granny Buzzard herself looked more like a wizened bird of paradise than a somber buzzard. What Annie Earle saw was a short, plump, little old woman layered in so many different pieces of clothing, she looked like a roof that had been shingled in leftover samples. The tattered remains of a lace tablecloth were gathered as a shawl around her shoulders. A blue velvet blouse, a red sash with fragments of gold fringe, three skirts of different lengths and colors, and a white ruffled petticoat flowed down to the floor, where the pointed toes of a pair of gray high-button shoes peeked out like two curious mice. Granny Buzzard's head was wrapped in a turban with material like the flowered print that hung in the doorway. A long black feather jutted at a rakish angle out of the turban. *It must be a buzzard's tailfeather*, thought Annie Earle.

The smoke cloud from the pipe cleared around Granny Buzzard's face, and Annie Earle was surprised again. Granny Buzzard was almost white. Her face looked like natural linen, a pale tan parchment color, as riddled with wrinkles as a dried white grape. Only her bright, piercing brown eyes escaped the wrinkle invasion. The toothless mouth and tiny button nose had long ago melted into the wrinkle mass. Annie Earle was thankful that her face was concealed behind the dark veils, so Granny Buzzard could not read her reactions.

"Rest yourselves," said Granny Buzzard, motioning toward a couple of orange crates before the fireplace.

"Thank you kindly," said Queen Esther.

Granny Buzzard made a cackling sound and said to Annie Earle, "You can rest your hat, too."

Queen Esther nudged Annie Earle when she hesitated to remove the hat. Then Annie Earle lifted the veils and laid the hat on her lap.

Granny Buzzard squinted through the wrinkles and studied Annie Earle for a good long time. It made Annie Earle edgy. She wanted to say something. She hadn't spoken a word since entering the cabin, but she remembered Queen's caution not to speak, so she said nothing.

"I'll need a drop of blood," said Granny Buzzard.

Annie Earle flinched.

"I need to take it from a place nobody can see," continued Granny Buzzard. "If you just lift your dress the knee will do fine."

Annie Earle looked at Queen Esther, who nodded. Then she slowly lifted her skirt, revealing first the clubfoot, then the knee.

"I see you been marked already," said Granny Buzzard. She came toward Annie Earle with a needle in her hand. Annie Earle closed her eyes and held her breath. She felt the tiniest little prick on her knee, then something soft pressed against the spot. She opened her eyes and saw Granny Buzzard examining a small scrap of white cloth with a scarlet stain in the shape of a spider on it.

"First signs be good," muttered Granny Buzzard. "Your blood pattern made a strong sign. Strong enough to cast a powerful spell. Now I must pose you three questions. And I want true answers. Just nod your head. No words must pass between us. You understand me?"

Annie Earle nodded.

"Somebody trying to do you harm?"

She nodded.

"Be there any evil intent on your part?"

She shook her head.

"If I make you a conjure bag, do you believe it will work?"

Annie Earle held still. She was afraid to move her head. In truth she didn't know the answer to the third question.

Granny Buzzard waited for a sign, but Annie Earle sat motionless. Queen Esther fidgeted with her fingers.

Granny Buzzard turned her back on them and said, "I got all the ingredients for what you need but one. I make you a conjure bag, but one thing gone be missing. You got to put that in. You got to put in your own faith. You wasting my time and your money if you don't believe."

"Annie Earle trying to believe," said Queen Esther. "All she need is the conjure bag and a little time to come to believing."

Granny Buzzard turned to face the girls. "Wait. It don't take but a minute to whip up a conjure bag." She shuffled behind a curtained area at the back of the cabin.

"I'm sorry," whispered Annie Earle. "I was afraid to lie to her and say I believed in the conjure bag, because I'm not sure I do."

"She gone make it, anyhow," said Queen Esther. "Maybe when you get it in hand, it be easier to believe."

"When do I give Granny Buzzard the money?"

"Take it out now. Put it in your hand. When Granny give you the bag, shake hands with her and leave the money in her palm."

The girls listened to the small noises coming from behind the curtain: the tinkle of jar lids, the dull, rhythmic scraping sound of grinding something with a pestle, the rustle of dried herbs.

"I just can't believe this place is real," Annie Earle whispered to Queen.

"What did you expect?" asked Queen.

"I expected a dirty, terrible-smelling, scary old shack, with a witch woman who looked like a buzzard."

"Most folks is scared of Granny Buzzard," whispered Queen. "But not for them reasons."

The curtains opened suddenly and Granny Buzzard tottered out. She was holding a small bag tied with a string.

"Here, child," she said, thrusting the bag forward.

Annie Earle took the bag with her left hand, and extended her right hand to shake Granny Buzzard's hand. The five-dollar-bill exchange was made.

Queen Esther stood up and handed Annie Earle the veiled hat. Annie Earle placed the bag in her pocket, put on the hat, and adjusted the veils to cover her face. She leaned toward Queen and whispered in her ear, "Ask her what I'm supposed to do with the bag."

"Pardon, Granny Buzzard," said Queen Esther, "but Miss Annie Earle wants to know what to do with the conjure bag."

Granny Buzzard cackled again. "You'll know when the time comes. You'll know as clear as rainwater." Then the old woman sat down and put the pipe back in her mouth. The session was over.

Queen Esther guided Annie Earle back through the dark maze of thick cedars. They hurried along as fast as Annie Earle's foot would allow, and to the relief of both of them, they encountered not a soul. They slipped quietly into the house and went to their separate rooms.

Annie Earle took the small bag from her pocket. It was the first chance she had had to look at it carefully. There was the red spider made from her own bloodstain. Granny Buzzard had used the piece of material with her blood on it to make the bag. The other ingredients were a complete mystery. The bag gave off a strange, unpleasant odor. *I can't sleep with this thing smelling up the room. Where will I put it?*

She walked slowly and quietly down the stairs to the parlor. The room was very dark, but she knew it well. She felt for the small table by the side of the fireplace, the Chinese cachepot with the painted dragon. She lifted the lid, and the stale perfume of dried rose petals rose from the cachepot. She burrowed through the soft petals and hid the conjure bag in the bottom of the pot.

I reckon it still needs one ingredient, she said to herself as she limped back up to her bedroom.

Cattail Bay

‹•···——◆——···•›

I can't believe you got to be this old and still don't know how to play checkers," exclaimed Queen Esther as she placed the bottle caps on the handmade game board.

A week had passed, and the girls had not spoken at all about the visit to Granny Buzzard's. They sat on the back porch, shaded from the afternoon sun that scorched the front of the house. Annie Earle was glad to take a break from the stifling heat in Mama's room. Aunt Charlotte battled the hot weather by opening the windows only at night and keeping the shades drawn during the day. The house looked as though it were suspended in a perpetual twilight, and the dark, still coolness trapped from the previous night held until late afternoon, when all of Aunt Charlotte's knowing ways could not defeat the invincible heat.

"It's so hot up there I don't see how Mama stands it. But when I try fanning her, she says the heat doesn't bother her."

"You want to play with the Coca-Cola caps or the Orange Crush?" asked Queen.

"Doesn't matter," answered Annie Earle.

"What you mean? It matters a lot. One kind of them playing caps be lucky for you. Which one you feel it be?"

"Aw, come on, Queen, you know it can't matter which kind I play with. I'm gonna be terrible, anyway."

"Sometimes I think you just too stubborn to let lucky

things happen to you. Go ahead and pick one, anyhow."

"All right, I like Orange Crush better than Coca-Cola, so I'll play with the orange caps."

"Whee! I be glad you picked the orange, 'cause my luck always be in the Coke caps. Now, first watch me set up my side of the board, then you just copy it on your side."

"Where'd you get this funny old board?"

"My friend Kitty Fisher made it for me. He real sharp player. Used to beat me all the time, but I be onto a lot of his tricks now, so he ain't beating me so bad lately."

"I've seen that Kitty Fisher pass the house on Saturdays, making deliveries from the ice plant. He looks mighty snappy, the way he wears that blue bandanna tied around his neck and that mannish cap pulled down over one eye."

"Yeah, Kitty's mannish all right. He been sniffing around my skirt tail since before he knowed what to do with what he might find!"

Annie Earle's flushed cheeks turned even redder. "Queen Esther, I don't know how to talk to you. You say the most scandalous things. Right out loud."

"What you mean, scandalous things? I be telling the truth. And I be even more surprised you ain't had some mannish little old boy sniffing around your skirt tail. Good-looking girl like you, all that pretty red hair and them nice love mountains pushing out there."

"Hush, Queen, you're embarrassing me to death. You've got me so flustered I'll never learn to play checkers."

Queen laughed and almost upset the checkerboard.

"What's so funny?"

"Never you mind," said Queen. "Now move one of your men."

While Annie Earle studied her move, they heard a rapping sound coming from an upstairs window. The girls looked up to see Aunt Charlotte at the window on the stair landing. When she saw she had their attention, she raised the window and called, "Is Brodie Lacewell down there?"

The girls shook their heads.

"I ain't seen him lately," said Aunt Charlotte. "When you all see him last?"

Neither girl could exactly remember.

"Look around downstairs and out in the garden," called Aunt Charlotte. "I'll look up here."

Anne Earle checked the garden, the front porch, and the side yards, while Queen Esther looked through the downstairs part of the darkened house.

By the time Annie Earle had circled the house, Aunt Charlotte and Queen Esther had met on the back porch.

"He must have wandered off. I just know it," said Aunt Charlotte. "That's all we need, have Brodie wandering off and Miss Kat accusing us not being fit to take care of him."

"If we didn't miss him asleep or nicktating somewhere in the house, I know where he is," said Annie Earle.

"Where, child?" asked Aunt Charlotte.

"Brodie always goes to the same place when I take him for a walk, to Cattail Bay to look for butterflies."

"What we waiting for?" asked Queen Esther. "It ain't more than ten minutes from here."

"Yes," said Aunt Charlotte distractedly. "You girls run over there, and I'll look through the house again and see after Miss Nel."

Queen Esther darted from the porch and shot across the street, while Annie Earle limped along after her as fast as she could. Halfway down the block, Queen paused and waited for her to catch up.

"Here, take my arm and hold on hard," she said to Annie Earle. "I'll get you there in ten minutes. You'll see."

Soon they were beyond the laid-out streets of the town and into a shaded patch of woods, following a wagon-track road that led to Cattail Bay. It was cooler in the dappled sunlight under the trees, and Queen speeded up. Annie Earle strained against her arm to keep apace, and Queen finally established a gait that they could both comfortably maintain.

"Brodie run away much?" asked Queen.

"Hardly ever. It's not like him. He's been good lately about staying inside the yard fence. Unless somebody goes with him." She panted for breath. "I don't know where else to look except Cattail Bay."

"We'll find him," said Queen Esther.

They pressed on, and in a few more minutes the trees began to thin out. Tall reeds and shaggy swamp willows bordered the path.

"Hang on," said Queen Esther. "We's almost there."

Pushing through the last few feet of reeds in the canebrake surrounding Cattail Bay, they stopped short in the blinding sunlight. Cattail Bay stretched before them like a large, shallow bowl, dry as a bone and filled with patches of green and brown cattails, dotted with great lavender blossoms of queen of the meadow, and blanketed underfoot with a carpet of golden-topped bitterweed. The brackish waters that flooded the basin during the winter dried out in the spring, and the place burst forth with glory after glory of wildflowers that lasted through summer and fall. It was an enchanted spot where butterflies came to linger.

Annie Earle shaded her eyes and scanned the bay. She cupped her hands and started to call out when suddenly she heard voices on the other side of the flowery basin. Queen Esther grabbed her arm and pulled her down behind a clump of cattails.

"That be them Callahan and Bullard boys."

"Yes, that's Bobo Bullard and his brother, and the Callahan twins. But why're you pulling me down? We could ask them if they've seen Brodie."

"I wouldn't ask them boys nothing. 'Specially out here in the middle of the woods. They's bad white trash."

"I know, but what are we going to do?"

"Keep low and find out what they's up to," replied Queen Esther. "And let's sneak up a little closer so we can hear what they saying."

Queen crawled through the thick golden-topped bitterweed to the next clump of cattails. Annie Earle followed.

"They's up to something. Just like I said. Betcha they's got a cat or some poor old dog they's worrying to death. Them's the ones tied a bunch of papers to a cat's tail and set it on fire, and all whooped and hollered to see that poor animal screaming and running crazy mad with pain."

They moved on to the shelter of the next clump of cattails. The voices grew clearer.

"Pull 'em down!"

"Bet there ain't no pecker at all in there!"

The boys were laughing and circling a tall clump of cattails.

"They's got something trapped behind them bushes," whispered Queen Esther.

"Yeah, pull them britches down!"

"Here, I'll do it for you!"

"Let's see if he's got a pecker in there!"

"Bet there ain't nothing inside his britches but a butterfly where his pecker oughta be!"

"Butterfly!" gasped Annie Earle. "Oh, my God, that's Brodie they're baiting. I'm going to him!"

By the time she had struggled to her feet, she saw Queen Esther dashing across the meadow with a dead branch in her hand. She moved with such speed she seemed to, be running on the golden tops of the bitterweed. Annie Earle plunged after her.

When the gang of boys turned to see the wild figure bearing down on them, Queen let out a chilling cry and crashed the last few feet to the clump of cattails that had concealed Brodie Lacewell from their view.

The boys were so taken by surprise that they backed off, and Queen quickly placed herself between Brodie and the gang. Brandishing the dead limb, she cried, "First one of you comes near's gonna get a busted head!"

Bobo Bullard pulled on his suspenders and grinned. "Well, well, look what else has turned up here in Cattail Bay."

"You better stand back, you big bully," yelled Queen.

"Ain't this something," shouted one of the Callahan twins. "Brodie's got his own nigger girl to do his fighting."

Bobo motioned the others around himself. "Maybe we oughta find out what this sassy little bitch's got between *her* legs."

"If it's a butterfly, we oughta pry open its wings and see what's inside," said Bobo's brother.

Annie Earle cursed her lame foot as she pushed toward the gang. Then suddenly she realized: *They haven't seen me. If I can sneak up on them, I can surprise them and draw them off Queen and Brodie.*

She ducked down and carefully began circling toward the rear of the boys.

"I got just the tool for opening up butterfly wings,"

bragged Bobo. He took a step toward Queen Esther. His hand played around with the buttons on the placket of his britches.

"You filthy son of a bitch, you come any closer, I'll part your hair down to the skull with this limb!"

"Oh, ho, ho, you hear what she called you, Bobo?" shouted one of the Callahan twins.

"Sassy bitch's got a nasty mouth, too," said the tall, lanky Bobo. "Well, I got just the thing to change her tune." He ripped open the buttons on the fly of his britches, exposing himself.

"You better get back," cried Queen.

Bobo's hands stretched forward, and he squatted slightly and rocked from side to side, stalking his prey, waiting for the right moment to grab the swinging limb. The others closed around the sides.

Brodie Lacewell, who had been motionless and silent throughout, began a high-pitched wail, like the bleating of a small animal in mortal peril.

Bobo edged forward, still crouched, making fake lunges toward the swinging stick. With a bold thrust and a loud triumphant grunt, he seized the swinging limb and held on. Queen Esther, still clutching the limb and shaking the tall boy hanging on to the end of it, screeched a horrible cry of rage and fear.

Bobo steadied himself, laughed, and began pulling the stick toward himself. Queen held on as if she had no power to let go of the limb. She screamed again. Then she lost her grip, plunged backward against the bleating Brodie Lacewell, and fell into the bitterweed.

At that moment Annie Earle sprang forward, knocking Bobo to the ground. She straddled the prone Bobo and seized his neck with both hands. "I'll kill you! I'll kill you!" she hissed into the red and choking face that stared up at her in utter amazement.

The sudden attack from behind them threw everyone into confusion for a moment. Queen Esther recovered first, and with lightning speed put herself between the gang and Annie Earle.

"Stay back," she warned, swinging the limb at the boys.

"She's killing him," cried Bobo's brother.

"Stay back!" screamed Queen Esther.

"His tongue's sticking out. She's choking him to death! Stop her," pleaded the brother.

"Annie Earle! Annie Earle!" Queen Esther shouted. "That's enough. Let him go. They ain't gonna give us no more trouble now."

Annie Earle pulled her hands from the throat of the gagging boy and pushed herself to a standing position. Queen Esther backed up to her and relaxed the swinging stick.

Standing in a cowed bunch, the boys watched Bobo struggle to his feet, coughing and spitting phlegm from his bruised throat. Tiny specks of golden bitterweed dotted his matted hair. He wobbled to the safety of the circle of boys and hung on to two of them while he retched. Wiping his mouth and nose on his shirt sleeve, he turned and faced Annie Earle. "You ever cross my path again, I'll git you. I'll get you and your nigger friend, Old Crooked Foot," he threatened. Then he struck the head of a tall queen of the meadow from its stalk. Lavender petals exploded in the air, floating toward the ground, and settled on the low bitterweed carpet of gold as the gang slunk out of Cattail Bay.

When the girls turned to check on Brodie Lacewell,

they saw him lying in the bitterweed, his body jerking in small spasms.

"Oh, my God! They must have hurt him bad," said Queen Esther.

"Quick, break me a stick off that limb," cried Annie Earle. "I've got to put something in his mouth so he don't chew his tongue. Brodie's having one of his fits. I don't think the boys hurt him."

After she got the stick between Brodie's teeth, Annie Earle sat on the ground with his head raised on her lap. "It'll pass in a minute," she said. "He won't even remember it."

Brodie ground his teeth on the stick while the spasm racked his body. True to Annie Earle's prediction, it lasted only a minute. He coughed and spit out the stick and began making little bleating cries again. The girls lifted him up. With their arms on his shoulders, they stood on either side of him until the small spasms and bleating cries ceased.

"We're going home now, Brodie," said Anne Earle. "That was a bad mare for all of us."

"Is that what it was?" asked Brodie.

"Yes, that's what it was," said Annie Earle. "Just a mare, and it's all over now."

Brodie accepted Annie Earle's explanation. In a few minutes he was running ahead of them on the woods road, exploring the plant and insect life, giving Annie Earle and Queen Esther their first chance to talk about the happening in Cattail Bay.

"I ought to go right down to the police station and report this whole thing," said Annie Earle.

"You crazy? That Bobo's uncle be one of the police-men. You ain't gone get me to swear nothing at that police station. You seems to forget I be colored. I'll settle my 'counts in my own way."

"I'd do it in a minute, if I could bring myself to tell everything that happened. But I know I could never say those things before anybody. I'd die of shame. I don't know how in the world I'm ever going to tell even Aunt Charlotte."

"Who says you gonna tell Gramma Charlotte?"

"Well, we've got to tell somebody."

"How come?"

"Queen, you can't let a thing like that happen and not tell somebody."

"We've got each other to talk to. Now, you listen to me, Annie Earle. Them good-for-nothing boys ain't gonna breathe a word of this. And Brodie already thinks it be a mare. You think careful what Gramma Charlotte said before we left the house. Your kin be just looking for something to take over legal. This could be all your aunt Kat needs."

Annie Earle limped along, quietly thinking over what Queen Esther had just said.

"It's wrong that way, Queen. It's not right. I hate this whole town. It's not right."

"You got to learn something I knowed a long time, Annie Earle."

"What's that?"

"You got to learn that the wrong thing can sometime be the right thing to do."

"I may learn it, but I'm never going to like it."

"It ain't so bad when you got a friend to chew it over with," said Queen.

As they entered the back gate, their long shadows stretched across the yard, heralding the coolness that would soon follow the waning strength of the setting sun. Aunt Charlotte waited on the porch.

"Thank God, you found Brodie. I was beside myself, you was gone so long."

"He was right where I said," explained Annie Earle.

Aunt Charlotte sniffed the air. "You all smells like quinine. You been wallowing around in bitterweed, I bet."

"Cattail Bay's full of bitterweed," said Queen Esther. "Yeah, we horsed around a little."

"Sometimes I think you girls be pretty growed up, other times you act like you still young'uns. All of you, get in here and wash that bitter smell off before supper."

As they passed in front of her to enter the house, Aunt Charlotte asked, "Brodie, what you got balled up in your fist there?"

Before Aunt Charlotte could get an answer, Annie Earle and Queen Esther grabbed Brodie by the arms and ran giggling into the house. "Come on, Brodie," cried Annie Earle.

"Last one to get the bitterweed stink off is a rotten egg," shouted Queen Esther.

When they were safely inside the darkened hall, they stopped. Brodie held out his clenched hand and opened it slowly, as though it was stiff from being balled up so long. Pale lavender wings lay crushed in his palm. "They didn't get my butterfly," he said.

The Oath

······ ◆ ······

After the curious trip to Granny Buzzard's, Annie Earle began sleeping very deeply. The nightmares stopped. The summer weather brought on heavy, eye-swelling sleep that kept her in bed until Queen Esther shook her shoulder and called her name.

"Grits is cold, and your eggs is turning to rubber," she said, trying to rouse Annie Earle. But Annie Earle rolled over and hid in the bed covers.

"I don't know what's come over you lately. You usually out of bed at first crack of dawn, checking on Miss Nel."

"Mama's fine," mumbled Annie Earle.

"How you know?"

"I can feel she's fine. I just don't wake up with that worry anymore. But I do feel heavy and real sleepy. My legs get cramps, and I feel like they weigh a ton."

She slid to the edge of the bed and pushed her feet and legs over the side.

"Good Lord!" exclaimed Queen Esther. "No wonder your legs feels heavy. They's swollen."

Annie Earle looked down at her feet. Her ankles were puffed out, and the top of her twisted foot was firmly rounded. She stood up. Her feet didn't really hurt. They just felt leaden and slightly numb.

"We better let Gramma Charlotte take a look at that swelling."

"They've been a little puffed up before," said Annie

Earle. "But it goes away when I stir around a bit."

"Still want Gramma Charlotte to take a look."

Aunt Charlotte didn't like what she saw. "I don't trust swellings when I can't see the cause. A bee sting, or bruise, or a cut I can vouch for. But I don't see no cause for that swelling in your ankles and feets. I 'spect Dr. Whittaker ought to take a look at you."

"Aunt Charlotte, you and Queen Esther are making a whole big to-do out of this. I'm fine. And I'm hungry. I want some pancakes and lots of syrup this morning."

Aunt Charlotte mumbled something the girls didn't catch and started whipping up the pancakes.

"Where's Brodie?" asked Annie Earle.

"He had his breakfast already. I last saw him out back by the gazebo," said Queen Esther.

"Well, we need to keep an eye on him this morning. Mr. Sears is sending someone over from the bank to help Mama. And she wants me and Brodie both in her room when he comes. It'd be just like Brodie to be off nicktating when he gets here."

"I'll go find Brodie while you having your pancakes."

They were gathered in Mama's room. Mama was on her chaise, looking real pretty in her pink silk dressing gown with the ecru lace. Her cheeks were a little flushed. Annie Earle wondered how much medicine Mama had taken.

Brodie Lacewell and Annie Earle sat on the small, straight-backed slipper chairs. Mr. Jack Cato sat in the armchair, well away from the back, as if poised to spring. Annie Earle was surprised at how young he appeared.

"We're putting our trust in you, Mr. Cato," said Mama. "That means we're going to be very straightforward. No holding back. Mr. Sears tells me you're honest, smart, and sharp as a sandspur. I know your family, even if I don't know you. Poor, but good stock, solid farmers. Now, sharp as a sandspur is what we need. You'll be acting for a pretty weak bunch. I'm practically helpless. Dear, sweet Brodie Lacewell is—well, mostly Brodie's somewhere else. Annie Earle is afflicted, as you can see."

Annie Earle winced at the word *afflicted. Why does Mama have to use that word? I don't feel afflicted. I wish she hadn't said that before Mr. Jack Cato.*

Mama continued. "Now, you see I haven't minced any words describing your clients, Mr. Cato. Here we are, a pretty pitiful group, the last of our line, about to be swallowed up by my avaricious sister, Katherine. If she gets power of attorney over us, I know well what she'll do."

Mama paused and patted her cheeks with a silk handkerchief. "Kat would put my children in religious institutions. She's said that's where they belong many a time. Well, I'll not have it as long as there's breath in me. Mr. Roland left us well fixed. If he hadn't left us a considerable estate, I doubt we'd be getting any problems from my sister Kat. Do you understand what I'm getting at, Mr. Jack Cato?"

"Indeed I do, Mrs. Roland. Mr. Sears merely gave me the facts. But I do appreciate your being so frank with me. It helps to know what's behind the facts. It gives one quite an advantage."

"I hear you've read law with Mr. Henderson," said Mama.

"Yes, ma'am, I clerked for Mr. Henderson for five years. Just passed the law bar this spring. Now I'm a full-fledged attorney myself."

"Then you know my sister Kat has retained Powell and Powell as her attorneys."

"Yes, ma'am, Powell and Powell are top dog in the legal pound around here. But they can't touch you as long as you don't, of your own free will, give consent," said Jack Cato.

"Well, right at this moment Sister Kat thinks she's got my consent. You sure there's no tricky way those Powells can take over without my signed consent?"

"Hardly. Unless they proved something on the order of insanity," answered Jack Cato.

"Kat wouldn't hesitate to try that."

"I figured as much from what Mr. Sears told me. So I've already done some shoring up."

"What do you mean?"

"I went to see Dr. Whittaker yesterday. The old doc was perfectly willing to certify that you are in your right mind and competent. Just a little piece of insurance I thought we could start with."

"My, you *are* a sandspur, Mr. Cato," said Mama with a smile.

Annie Earle smiled, too. *A piece of insurance. Mr. Jack Cato must have been reading my mind. That's just what I've been looking for. Now we've got two pieces of insurance, counting Granny Buzzard's conjure bag.*

Annie Earle studied the young man. He was average height, thin and wiry, with a long, straight nose set in a sharp face. Close-cropped blue-black curls softened the sharpness. Small, round, and sparkling black eyes seemed to be checking everything in his line of vision. He had large hands for his size. She remembered Mama had said he was from farming stock. It showed in his hands. He still sat in the big armchair like a coiled spring, ready to jump in a split second. It struck Annie Earle that his name ought to be Jack Cat, not Cato. There really was something about him that reminded her of a smart cat. She felt a surge of reassurance. This smart cat was on their side. A smart young cat could probably stand up pretty well against an old vulture.

Mama and Jack Cato were still talking. "I'll bring the proper papers, and when they're signed I'll be authorized as power of attorney to handle all your business affairs for the fees we've agreed on. That gives me a vested interest in your estate, Mrs. Roland, and that's a strong incentive to keep others, such as your sister, from meddling. Your main job is to keep well. Your children are still minors. You just work at keeping well, Mrs. Roland. I'll take care of the rest."

Suddenly Annie Earle's old fear rushed back to sit like a knot in her throat. A lot still depended on poor frail Mama. Jack Cat might be in a pickle if anything happened to Mama. Dr. Whittaker's certification was a reprieve. But who could tell for how long.

When Mr. Jack Cato took his leave, he shook hands all around. He held Annie Earle's hand a mite longer than the others as he explored her face with those sparkling black eyes. It was very reassuring to the Rolands to feel his strong, firm handshake. Even Brodie Lacewell made a comment without being asked a direct question. "Thank you, sir," he said. "I know we can trust you."

Annie Earle was astonished to see Brodie escort Mr. Cato out of the room, down the stairs, and to the front door. A faint hope flickered. *Maybe Brodie's changing. Dr. Whittaker said we might see some changes when Brodie got to be a teenager. But Brodie's already past sixteen. I'd pretty much given up looking for any changes.*

The next morning Annie Earle slept late again, so late that Queen Esther came to wake her. The swelling in her legs and ankles was much worse. The twisted foot was puffed like a balloon. When she put weight on it, a dull, throbbing pain shot up her leg.

Queen Esther watched her hobble across the room to a chair. "Well, I trust there ain't gonna be no arguments about seeing Dr. Whittaker today," she said.

Annie Earle was annoyed, but also a little frightened. "I'll go on condition," she snapped.

"What condition?"

"On condition that nobody tells Mama. She doesn't need any extra worries."

"You got your condition far as I'm concerned. And I 'spect Gramma Charlotte gone see it the same way."

"There's no need to bother Brodie, either," said Annie Earle.

She lumbered up the two short steps to the door marked "J. A. Whittaker, M.D." It was the second time within the week that Annie Earle had visited the old doctor.

Inside the small, empty waiting room, she plopped into a wicker chair and rested for a few moments to control her shortness of breath. Then she called, "Doc, you still here?"

In the past few years the old doctor had become ancient, along with most of the patients he attended. Annie Earle was one of the youngest he still saw.

After Annie Earle's second call, he came tottering out of his private office, rubbing his eyes and yawning. "Nothing but the truth for Annie Earle. I learned that while you were still a slip of a girl. So, truthfully, I was napping."

"You've earned your naps, Doc," she replied. "Well,

here I am, right on time. Did you get those test reports back?"

"Matter of fact, they came in this morning."

"All right, then, Doc, give it to me straight. What's wrong?"

"Annie Earle, you're a borderline diabetic. It's something we've got to watch. We certainly don't want it to develop into full-fledged diabetes."

"What does that mean, Doc?"

"It gives me some of the answers to why your circulation is so poor in the legs, especially in your right foot. And it accounts for the swelling and muscle cramps you have from time to time in the legs."

"Well, now that we've got that accounted for, what do we do, Doc?"

"Unfortunately, there's not much *I* can do. Oh, I can give you some quinine for the muscle cramps. But there's a good deal *you* can do about your diet. And exercise will help. You've got to be careful about your weight, and you've got to get the circulation in your legs improved."

"What kind of diet?"

"Well, let's start with no sweets of any kind—no sugar at all—and no fats. That means no fried foods or butter. We'll see how it works."

"That's going to be harder on Aunt Charlotte than it is on me," said Annie Earle with a nervous laugh.

"There's more metal in you than I've been giving you credit for, Annie Earle. Now come on in and let me weigh you and check your blood pressure."

Dr. Whittaker said he wanted to check her about once a month. And he reminded her that she needed to exercise and diet. Annie Earle knew she needed to think. Hard rocking-chair thinking was what she needed. But for exercise she decided to take a roundabout route home. *Try thinking while walking.*

Her thinking was as heavy as the swollen feet she doggedly dragged along. *Maybe you ought to join Mama and Brodie. Just slip into your own little world. Mama's got her pills and her couch. Brodie's perfectly happy in the realm of nicktation. Not much can touch them. Where would you go, girl? Who would look after Mama and Brodie? That's the catch. You don't have an out. Not one you can justify. Bad foot, borderline diabetes, and Aunt Kat could all be excuses, but they can't keep you down, girl. Annie Earle Roland, stop feeling sorry for yourself. Are you the fighter in this family or not?*

She felt better, relieved to know what was causing the swelling and pain in her legs. Suddenly walking didn't feel so burdensome. It was proving almost as good for thinking as her worry rocker.

She worked her way around the edge of town and out to the county fairgrounds. Except for the old wooden warehouse they called the Exhibition Hall, the fairground looked like a cow pasture. Annie Earle sat down on a sagging bench in front of the Exhibition Hall to catch her breath. She closed her eyes and tried to picture the place the way she remembered it the first time her mother and father had brought her there. The empty space had been filled with flags and bunting, carnival rides, freak shows, and prize booths—a fantasy world for one glorious week each year. The music from the hobby horses and the Ferris wheel, piping different tunes that blended in a feverish duet of toe-tapping excitement, came back to her in a rush.

She heard laughter. At first thinking it part of her imagining, she paid it no mind. But she heard it again, this time accompanied by footfalls coming from inside the old Exhibition Hall. She moved from the bench to the front door. It was slightly ajar. Annie Earle peeked in. Tommy Hickman, the boy who'd danced with every girl but her at the school dance, was kissing Peggy Davis, one of her former classmates. They were giggling and necking inside the Exhibition Hall. Right in the stall where they showed off the prize pigs.

Annie Earle flushed and pulled back. She felt embarrassed, mad, and jealous all at the same time. She step-slapped as fast as she could away from the fairgrounds, confused by her own mixed feelings.

She was sweaty and well worn out when she reached her backyard. And still irritable. Her eye was drawn to the gazebo. She saw Kitty Fisher plant a quick kiss on Queen Esther's cheek and bolt like a shot across the backyard. He cleared the hedge in a jack-rabbit leap and disappeared down the street.

Must be the kissing season, she thought as she moved toward the back door. *Well, it's not my season. None of that nonsense for you, Annie Earle. It's disgusting. You couldn't care less. Then why is it so irritating to see it going on all around you?*

She clumped into the kitchen. It was empty. Then she heard voices coming from the hall. Aunt Kat and Aunt Charlotte were coming down the stairs. It seemed as if she was forever meeting Aunt Kat on the staircase.

"I knew Penelope would pull one of those spells on me the moment I confronted her," Aunt Kat complained.

"She don't do it on purpose," said Aunt Charlotte.

"Well, she is smart enough to use it for her own purposes, let me tell you," quipped Aunt Kat.

Annie Earle met them at the bottom of the stairs.

"Is Mama all right?" she asked.

"Not in the head," snapped Aunt Kat. "She's not to be trusted for anything she says. Nel promised me weeks ago she'd sign the papers I had Powell and Powell send over. I've been patient and not pressured her. Now she's gone behind my back with that upstart Jack Cato. She's pushing me too far."

"I wish you wouldn't upset Mama," said Annie Earle.

"Upset Nel! Do you know what she's done to upset me? Here I am trying to do my best by her and you help-less children, and she knifes me in the back."

"Mama's just trying to look after our future," said Annie Earle.

"Future! What future? Nel's branch of our family has reached a dead end. It's the will of the Lord that it gets pinched off right here. Now, this may sound hard to you, Annie Earle, but I was never one to put frilly falsehoods around the truth to make it more palatable."

"Aunt Kat, don't talk like that! That's the meanest thing I've ever heard anybody say. I'm fifteen years old. I could marry and have lots of children and take care of Brodie, too."

"Ha! You must still be reading those fairy tales. Or maybe you've got a pet frog around the house that's going to turn into some sort of prince. Nonsense. Nel leaves me no alternative. I'm going to test this thing under the law. Powell and Powell assures me we can get her declared incompetent, if not insane. Everybody in this town knows the facts. I'd just hoped Nel still had sense enough to keep our dirty family linen in the closet."

"Aunt Kat, shut up! Mama's frail, but she's not crazy! I won't have you saying things like that about her!" Annie Earle realized what she had said, and to whom she had said it. She was shaking, but feeling glad she'd said it, anyway.

Aunt Kat pulled herself up, tall and stiff-necked. "No manners. Brought up by niggers and a dotty mother. It's

70

just the kind of disrespect I might expect from you, Annie Earle."

She crammed her black bonnet on her head and opened the front door. She turned back and said with a forced smile on her face, "For your sake, I hope I get control before it's too late to straighten you out." She slammed the door and left.

Annie Earle turned to Aunt Charlotte.

"Mama?"

"Too many pills. I don't know where she got them. Sometimes I think Miss Nel slips out at night and roams the house. I been keeping her pills in the kitchen ever since she had that bad spell."

Annie Earle went directly to Mama's room. She tiptoed over to the bed and looked down at the pale, pretty face framed in a tangle of black curly hair.

"You're more my child than I am yours," she whispered. "Sleep deep and peaceful, Mama. I, Annie Earle Roland, swear to keep this family together. Somehow, somehow. I swear it."

The Brickyard

For all her secret swearing, Annie Earle was not freed from her feelings of irritation. She was sharp with Brodie and short with Queen Esther and Aunt Charlotte. The fear of what Aunt Kat was stirring up behind her back slipped up and nipped at her at the most unexpected times.

At first the strict diet seemed to be working. The swelling in her legs and ankles went down. But when the full heat of summer settled in, the leaden feeling and the numbness returned. There were questions she wanted to put to Dr. Whittaker, but feared to ask.

Queen Esther told Annie Earle it would be good for her to get out of the house for a spell. "It be cool at the brickyard," promised Queen Esther as they walked along the dusty road carrying long reed poles over their shoulders. "And ain't no better time for fishing than just before dog days set in," she added.

"Are you telling me the fish don't bite during dog days?" asked Annie Earle with a laugh.

"Yeah, I'm telling you. Fish don't bite and sores don't heal and dogs run mad. Rattlesnakes bite without shaking they rattles to warn you. And people does crazy things."

"To hear you tell it, a person would be better off to hole up in the house and not come out till dog days were over. I'll settle for the fact that it's cool at the brickyard," said Annie Earle, shaking her heavy braids where they lay close and sweaty against the nape of her neck.

"Slow down, Queen, it's too hot to race. The fish will wait."

Queen Esther adjusted her gait to match the step-slap pace that was comfortable for Annie Earle.

"Did you give Kitty Fisher an answer yet?" asked Annie Earle.

"I usually gives Kitty Fisher a laugh instead of an answer."

"Is that what you gave him this time?"

"No, a laugh won't do no more. Kitty ain't playing around now the way we was when we was growing up. He means business this time."

"So what did you tell him?"

"I still give him a laugh, but I promise by Sunday I give him a real answer."

"Well, you know I want you to do what makes you happy, Queen, but I'd more than hate to see you go out of our house. Maybe you can still help out Aunt Charlotte."

"You acting like I already made up my mind."

"Don't you love Kitty Fisher?"

"Course I do. But I ain't as hot to go jumping between the bed covers with legal sanction as Kitty Fisher be."

"I swear, Queen, if we live to be hundred-year-old friends, I don't think you'll ever stop shocking me."

"Well, how would you feel if some good-looking man was pressing you like that?"

"I don't know," answered Annie Earle softly. "I don't know. Nobody ever tried."

"Shoot, they will, you'll see."

Queen Esther and Annie Earle walked on without talking for a few moments.

"It's not how much I love Kitty Fisher," mused Queen out loud. "I be just as hot for him as he be for me. I just don't let it show. Trouble is, the thought of getting pinned down cools me right off. In truth, it scares me to death."

"What do you mean?"

"Now, don't you laugh, Annie Earle. I can't be cooped up. I got to fly."

"I hope Kitty Fisher understands what you're talking about better than I do."

"It ain't the kind of feeling I could ever talk to Kitty about. But it be the kind I get when Kitty presses me too close."

"Well, what kind of feeling have you got about catching fish today?"

Queen Esther swung the bait bucket she was carrying in a wide circle over her head, then brought it to rest in the dust at her feet without losing a single fat earthworm.

"Fish is gonna grab our baits today!" she cried.

Entering the brickyard, Annie Earle felt like an explorer coming upon the remains of a long-lost city. Broken walls of stacked red bricks, sun bleached and aged into hues of pink and rose, surrounded a large oval body of water. Honeysuckle vines tangling with Virginia creeper, smilax, and poison cow itch wound and snaked their way over the stacks of flaking bricks like the handiwork of a mad wrapper. Lizard and bug life abounded in the cool crevasses between the brick. With its feeder stream dried up, the pond lay still and sluggish, shimmering in the quiet hush of places long deserted.

But Annie Earle recalled the site when the brickyard was alive with industry. Mr. Roland had brought her there when she was five, and the memory of sweating black men naked to the waist, standing ankle deep in the shallow water at one end of the pond, hacking out clay for new bricks, remained sharp and clear. The great green-covered mounds of crumbling bricks were once live rumbling kilns with glowing furnaces and firestacks belching clouds of white smoke. The broken, vine-covered walls were the remnants of the remembered labyrinth of neatly stacked rows of new-made bricks through which she had wandered with her father a childhood ago.

"Looks like we're the only ones here," said Annie Earle.

"Shh, shh," cautioned Queen Esther. "Don't make no fuss till we get our hooks baited. Big, fat brim lays close to the edges when it's quiet and still."

Annie Earle sat on a low pile of crumbling bricks and baited her line with a long, squirming Georgia jumper.

"That ought to be an attractive offering," she whispered.

"A little wiggling action do help," answered Queen Esther with a smothered giggle.

As they eased to the water's edge with baited lines, Queen Esther reached over and lowered the cork on Annie Earle's line. "We start fishing shallow till they scared off and goes into deep water," she whispered.

Barely breaking the smooth sheen of the pond, they slipped their lines into the water and watched the wiggling Georgia jumpers sink out of sight under the pull of the lead sinkers. The corks made a single bobbing movement, signaling that the bait had reached its depth, then they settled expectantly on the surface.

Annie Earle and Queen Esther watched the two corks intently, prepared to react to the slightest movement. But minutes passed, and the lazy corks never stirred.

"You sure these fish know it's still some time before dog days?" asked Annie Earle.

Queen Esther jiggled her line in a wide arc. "Maybe they's asleep and need a little stirring up."

"I was thinking while we were watching the corks," said Annie Earle. "I was thinking these corks are a lot like you and me, Queen. We're just sitting and waiting for something to happen to us. And we don't know what's down there where we've put out our bait. But I reckon that's what most people do. Just wait and see what happens and hope for the best."

"You right. Most people just takes whatever comes along. But you know something, Annie Earle, me and you ain't *most people.*"

Queen jerked her line out of the water and brought the bait up close to her face. Then she spit on the water-logged Georgia jumper and plopped the line back into the water.

"Why'd you do that?" asked Annie Earle.

"Supposed to be good luck. I ain't the kind to do a lot of wait and see. And I ain't the kind to just take whatever comes along. I think that be the thing in me that's tying me up in knots about my answer to that sweet, loving Kitty Fisher."

"In a way I know what you mean," replied Annie Earle. "I've felt different from other people as long as I can remember. And I never minded that. What I mind is a scary feeling I get sometimes that I'm going to live and die and nothing important is ever going to happen to me."

"You talking junk, Annie Earle. And you don't sound like my special friend when you talk like that. It's just like fishing. You shake that pole around, and you spit on that worm, and you twist and turn things about. But you ain't the kind to just sit by—"

Queen's cork bobbed dizzily and streaked off at an angle into the deep water.

"See what I mean!" she yelled. "Fat brim's striking."

With a wide swing of the reed pole, Queen Esther landed a glistening fish. While she shrieked and exclaimed over the fine catch, Annie Earle quickly pulled her bait from the water, spit on it, and returned it to the pond without letting Queen see what she had done. Miraculously, her cork shot downward into the water and she landed a gleaming silver fish.

Queen was busy dipping a bucket of water to keep her catch fresh. The silvery fish flipped off the hook and lay tangled in the honeysuckle vines at the base of a pile of bricks. Anne Earle limped over to pick up her catch. "Look!" she cried. "Isn't this a beauty?"

Queen Esther turned and looked at the glistening fish in Annie Earle's hand.

"Yeah, you caught a good looker. But he ain't worth nothing for eating. That's a shiner. They spoils before you can get 'em home. They's full of bones, anyhow. Best thing to do with a shiner is admire him and throw him back."

Disappointed, Annie Earle gave the fish a mighty fling and sent the shiner flashing through the air like a miniature comet. It landed with a splash far out in the pond.

"Quick, bait your hook," said Queen. "They's hungry now."

In half an hour they had caught a half-dozen fat brim.

"Don't that water look nice and cool," said Queen Esther. "We's got enough fish for a good mess. Sure would be nice to cool off in the water. It do your feet and legs good, too."

"We didn't bring our bathing outfits," said Annie Earle.

"Ain't nobody here. How come we need bathing outfits?"

"Well, how can we go in?"

"You ever hear of naked?"

"Good Lord, I couldn't. Not even before you, Queen. I couldn't."

"Well, I could before you. There ain't nothing to be ashamed of."

"It sure looks nice and cool, but I just couldn't."

"Well, what's wrong with your petticoat? You could go in with your petticoat and save your drawers and frock to wear home."

"But what if somebody came by?"

"You could melt in this heat, trying to think of all the 'what ifs' could happen. I'm going in and cool off."

Queen Esther began stripping off her clothes. Annie Earle was aghast when she slipped out of her petticoat and stood on the bank in only a pair of knee-length drawers.

"Queen Esther, stop! Don't you take off another stitch. Don't you wear a camisole?"

"Don't need one," replied Queen. "Here I go," she cried, and plunged into the water.

When she emerged from the dive with only her head above the water, she called out to Annie Earle. "Who could tell but what I be in a proper bathing outfit? Oh, it do feel good. You coming in?"

Annie Earle made no reply.

"Or you just gonna sit and wait for things to pass you by?" chided Queen.

Annie Earle began pulling off her clothes furiously, first the dress, then the underdrawers. And running her hands under her petticoat, she released her camisole and stood on the bank clad only in her thin cotton petticoat.

"Jump!" shouted Queen Esther.

She limped to the edge of the pond and flopped in with a belly buster.

When she surfaced, Queen Esther exclaimed, "Ain't this great?"

"It's delicious," Annie Earle conceded.

They played in the refreshing water, ducking each other and enjoying the sensation of cool wetness caressing the skin.

Queen Esther floated lazily on her back. "Try this," she said. "Just let go and feel yourself light as a feather."

Annie Earle looked at her slender friend with the thin, gauzy drawers billowing in a filmy cloud around gleaming golden limbs. Her face and naked breasts jutted out of the water, cutting a sharp clear outline in contrast to the soft focus of her body just below the surface of the water.

Why am I still nervous as a cat in water? Why can't I be like Queen Esther? Easy and free, floating with my breasts pointed toward the skies? Queen's so beautiful there in the water. It can't be wrong to be like that.

"Here goes," cried Annie Earle. She flipped onto her back and rose to the surface. "If I can stop holding my breath, I think I'll get it," she gasped.

"Light and easy. Don't fight it. Give in and the water will hold you up," Queen Esther said.

After a few minutes Annie Earle said, "I've got it. You're right. It feels good on my legs. I feel as lazy and light as that cloud up there looking down at me."

Queen Esther giggled. "You be a better floater than me," she said. "You got bigger water wings."

The grip of midsummer heat evaporated, and time seem suspended as they floated in the cool brickyard waters.

Suddenly a pebble plopped into the pond near Annie Earle. She lifted her head quickly and scanned the bank. Two grinning faces emerged from behind a stack of vine-covered bricks.

The white face puckered up and blew a long, suggestive whistle. It was Tommy Hickman. "You sure know how to pick fishing holes, Kitty Fisher," he said.

"Whoa, ho, ho," shouted Kitty Fisher. "Mermaids rising from the brickyard pond. This be a miracle!"

The girls sank to their necks in the water.

"Don't you go gaping at us," cried Queen Esther. "You just keep your distance till these miracles get dressed."

"Get back, Tommy Hickman," shouted Annie Earle. "Both of you get behind those bricks till we get dressed."

Kitty Fisher and Tommy Hickman ducked obediently behind a crumbling column of bricks.

The girls scrambled to the bank and grabbed their clothing. Annie Earle slipped her dress over her head and pulled it down before releasing her clinging petticoat. Queen Esther followed suit and wiggled out of her wet underdrawers. In a few minutes they had clothes on and water-soaked feet crammed into resistant shoes.

Annie Earle asked Queen, "What's Tommy Hickman doing fishing with Kitty?"

"Oh, they's been fishing together since they's little."

"You all dressed yet?" called Tommy Hickman.

"You can come out now," announced Queen Esther.

The grinning young men stepped from behind the pile of bricks.

"I'm gonna fix you good, Kitty Fisher," cried Queen Esther. She made a swipe at him with her wet underdrawers.

Kitty Fisher neatly dodged the stinging snap of the

drawers, then snatched them deftly from Queen Esther's hand. "You'll have to catch me first," he cried, swinging the trophy over his head and dashing into the maze of broken brick stacks. Queen shot after him. Their joyous laughter and playful shrieks bounced off the walls of the crumbling labyrinth.

Annie Earle was left alone with Tommy Hickman. "We didn't mean to break up your swim," he said. "The friendly thing would have been an invitation to join."

Annie Earle was completely flustered. She felt messy and uncomfortable. Water dribbled from her wet hair into her eyes. Tommy Hickman, who had never so much as said "hello," stood there leering at her. She blushed, hot and mad. "They've got a name for people like you, Tommy, who go around spying on folks."

"And they've got a name for good-looking girls like you who lure young men into dangerous waters," teased Tommy.

Annie Earle was uncertain how to respond. She'd known Tommy Hickman all through high school, and he'd never shown that he knew she existed. He was famous for playing the field with the girls, but Annie Earle had never been in the game. "You're welcome to go in if you want to," she replied.

"Well, it wouldn't be any fun all by myself. What about you and me taking a dip together?"

She felt nervous and excited at the same time. The playful sounds of Queen Esther and Kitty Fisher rang through the brickyard.

"I've got to dry my hair," she said, and began undoing a long, wet braid.

"I could help you," Tommy said, reaching for the other braid.

Annie Earle felt a deep flush rising from her bosom,

moving up her neck and into her cheeks. He was practically breathing on her ear as he unwound the braid. He spoke very softly. "You know, Annie Earle, you've changed. I don't know why I've never noticed you before."

"I'd say you've always been too busy noticing a half-dozen other girls."

He finished unwinding the braid and began running his fingers through her long, wet hair. He brushed his lips against her ear. "You've got beautiful hair, you know."

"It's all wet," she replied as she pulled away from him. She liked the feel of his hands in her hair and his lips on her ear, but there was something about him that made her ill at ease.

Tommy followed and stood close behind her. "It's a little crowded here at the brickyard today. You know what I mean, with Kitty and Queen Esther. Why don't we set a time, and I'll take you fishing. Just the two of us. Maybe we could go swimming, too?"

He slid his hand onto her shoulder. Annie Earle turned to face him. "What do you take me for, Tommy Hickman?" she stammered. "If there's anything to this talk I'm hearing from you, there's a better way to prove it."

"You name the way, baby, and I'm your man."

She was thrown again by Tommy's fast banter. No boy had ever talked to her like this before. She wiped her face with the back of her hand, trying to think how to reply. "Well, we don't start with fishing and swimming."

"You just tell old Tommy where to start."

"We start on my front porch in a couple of rockers on Sunday afternoon."

Tommy looked trapped. "Anything you say. Just set the time and I'll be there."

"Four o'clock," said Annie Earle, amazed that she had

made a date with Tommy Hickman. And, having done it, she wanted to run away as quickly as possible. "I've got to find Queen Esther. We've got to get home."

They followed the sounds of laughter and found Kitty and Queen Esther behind one of the large, crumbling kilns. Kitty had Queen penned against a stack of bricks. She was giggling and protesting, but not trying to free herself.

"Give up?" said Kitty.

"I surrender!"

Kitty Fisher planted a long, nuzzling kiss at the base of her throat. His arms closed around her, and he held her close. Queen did not resist him, but neither did she seek his nearness with her arms.

Annie Earle felt herself flushing deeply as she witnessed the scene.

Queen wiggled free from Kitty's embrace. He looked at her longingly and said, "I be waiting for my answer."

Annie Earle cleared her throat and called out, "Queen, I think we ought to be getting on. I promised to sit with Mama some this afternoon."

The boys walked with them to where the road forked and led back into town.

"We'll go the rest of the way home by ourself," said Queen Esther. "No need to give nosy folks the pleasure of gossiping about what we may or may not be up to."

They laughed and parted. When they were only a few yards apart, Kitty Fisher threw his cap into the air, jumped to catch it, and yelled.

The girls turned to look.

"Sunday! Don't you forget!" called Kitty.

Tommy Hickman winked broadly at Annie Earle and said, "Ditto!"

"I think they's already running crazy with the dog day

blues," said Queen Esther. She looked at Annie Earle. "What that Tommy Hickman mean?"

"Oh, I don't know. Just some silly talk, I reckon."

Dressed in her Sabbath best, Annie Earle wandered aimlessly through the darkened house that lay so hushed on Sunday afternoons. With Aunt Charlotte off visiting a sick grandchild, Queen Esther buggy riding with Kitty Fisher, Brodie holed up in his room with cotton and alcohol and knife and pins, meticulously mounting butterflies, and Mama dozing on her chaise, the ambient noises that gave the old house its regular pulse were stilled. Annie Earle's step-slap footfalls echoed loudly as she moved from room to room.

She found herself standing in the musty-smelling dining room. It was a dead room, unused since Mr. Roland passed away and Mama started taking her meals upstairs. But Aunt Charlotte kept it dusted and oiled and ready for use. The sickly sweet smell of stale air and rose oil furniture polish filled her nostrils, making the stifling heat unbearable in the room.

On into the parlor she moved, and over to the cachepot with the painted dragon. Her fingers traced the length of the dragon's red-and-gold scaly body. She lifted the lid and dug through the dried rose petals. Her fingers touched the conjure bag. It felt warm and damp, alive, as if something were starting to germinate, as if some hidden life force were beginning to stir in the dead, dry rose petals. She jerked her hand from the cachepot and replaced the lid.

Stop it, Annie Earle, you're letting your imagination grab you. There's nothing in that pot to scare you.

But her thoughts were poor reassurance. She quickly left the parlor and headed for the front porch, knowing that it was still an hour away from four o'clock and Tommy Hickman's arrival.

At least the air was fresher on the porch, and the shaded spot behind the Virginia creeper vines always felt cooler. She sat in her thinking rocker and gently moved to and fro. She rested her head against the high back of the chair, closed her eyes, and tried not to think at all. But the thoughts crept in, coming in sneaky little snatches, fragments, bits of free-floating images.

Tommy Hickman . . . girls chasing after him all the time . . . never thought that game was for me . . . other girls but not me . . . always looking on from the outside . . . I counted myself out before it started. Good-looking Tommy running after me . . . sure didn't encourage him. Annie Earle, stop fooling yourself. You know what kind of offer he was making you. Queen Esther would call his number "a hot buck panting at the swimming hole." Well, I didn't fall for that one. But you did feel something, girl, there's no denying that.

The rhythm of the rocker slowed and died. She dozed in the chair in the cool refuge behind the sheltering porch vines.

When she woke her first thought was *How late is it?* She limped to the front door and peered in at the old hall clock standing by the stair landing. The hands stood at ten minutes till four. She moved inside the hallway and checked her hair in the wall mirror. No, she hadn't mussed it too badly. It surely looked nicer than when he'd seen it and admired it at the brickyard. She smoothed the lap wrinkles on the front of her pretty dress of white lawn and lace.

Annie Earle returned to the porch and moved the chair so she would be visible from the street. Then she sat down, feeling a little nervous and hoping she wouldn't start beading up with perspiration.

. . .

At six-thirty, when Queen Esther returned, she found Annie Earle sitting on the front porch.

"Where's everybody?" asked Queen. "Did Gramma Charlotte get back yet?"

Annie Earle rocked slowly. "Not yet," she answered softly.

"What you be doing all dressed up? You expecting somebody?"

"Can't a person put on a decent dress on Sunday without expecting somebody?" Annie Earle snapped.

"Oh, ho, ho. You's hiding something, Annie Earle. I can tell."

"Queen, there's nothing in my life to hide. That's the trouble. I wish I had something worth hiding."

"You acting mighty strange," said Queen Esther. She walked over and laid a hand on Annie Earle's forehead. "No, cool as a cucumber, but you still acting in a strange way. And me here just busting to tell you something."

"I'm sorry, Queen. You and Kitty Fisher are going to get married. Is that what you're busting to tell me?"

"It's about Kitty, all right. Oh, I do feel good. I feel so good, I feel like I could flap my arms and fly right off this porch."

"When's it going to be, Queen?"

"I don't know when I'm gonna fly off, but now I know I can."

"Queen, what are you talking about?"

"Oh, that Kitty Fisher be a loving man, but, better, he be a understanding one. He see my path when I explained it to him, and he set me free. I know it hurt him deep, but he set me free."

"You'll drive me crazy, Queen, if you don't tell me what you're talking about."

"I'd made up my mind if I couldn't explain it to Kitty Fisher, I'd say yes and marry him, and try as hard as I could fight what's in me to be a good wife to him. And I left this house thinking, Kitty'll never know what I be talking about. But Kitty knows me deeper than I thought. He set me free. We ain't getting married. Oh, I wish I could just hand you a chunk of this good feeling I'm so full of."

Queen Esther walked over to Annie Earle and picked up her hands. "Now, I told you what lays closest to my heart. But you still ain't told me what's bothering you."

"I was stood up. On my first date," blurted Annie Earle.

"What date you be referring to?"

"Tommy Hickman. He asked when we were at the brickyard to come sit with me this Sunday."

Queen Esther released her hands and stepped back to look directly at Annie Earle. "You remember that shiner you caught at the brickyard? That's what Tommy Hickman be, honey, just a good-looking shiner. You's lucky he didn't get tangled on your hook."

"You're right, Queen. I know you're right, but I sure would have liked the pleasure of hooking him, even if I decided to throw him back."

Achilles McPherson

◆

It was hot. The sagging part of August dog days' heat had settled in, moist and steamy. No wonder dogs went rabid and sores wouldn't heal. Dog days were trying times, uncertain times, dangerous times.

Aunt Kat was too quiet. Jack Cato was too confident. Nobody was making a move, and it made Annie Earle uneasy. On the surface everything seemed suspended for the duration of dog days. But Annie Earle knew it wasn't true. The conjure bag in the cachepot was stirring, just like the dog days' mildew that crept in silently, unnoticed until it spotted everything with moldy gray spores.

Annie Earle thumped down the front walk—*step-slap, step-slap*—to the picket fence that separated their yard from the sidewalk. Maybe a little air was stirring along the open street. She leaned against the picket fence and faced away from the sun. With half-closed eyes she stood for a few moments watching the specks of light she called dazzle angels bouncing off the silvery sidewalk pavement.

"I wonder if everyone sees these sunstruck angels flitting in and out during August dog days," she said to herself, rubbing her eyes to make them vanish. They only darted faster and changed to shocking colors after the eye rub. Usually the dazzle angels were a silvery, transparent color, dancing in and out with hypnotic repetition. Now they were exotic pinks, purples, and blues, wild and erratic.

Wouldn't it be great if Brodie could collect dazzle angels instead of butterflies, thought Annie Earle. *I must remember to ask Queen Esther how to catch them.*

Behind her and coming from the direction of the sun, Annie Earle heard footfalls. A strange tingling set up in the back of her neck. She passed her hand underneath her long, deep red hair at the nape of her neck to let in a little air where the tingling played. The footfalls drew nearer. The tingling raced down her back, shot along her hips, and settled in the calves of her legs. She shifted her weight and shook first her good leg, then the weak one.

Annie Earle turned to face the sun and there, bearing down on her, was a strange young man with mane aflare in the relentless light and eyes as cool and green as new spring lettuce. He was too big and too near to be a dazzle angel. And he stood there solid and real, despite the halo bouncing off him in the hot glare of a cruel August dog-day sun.

The sun god spoke: "Morning, ma'am. My name's Achilles McPherson."

"Pleased to meet you," stammered Annie Earle. She raised a hand to her forehead to shield her eyes from the glare. The young man failed to evaporate. The tingling in her legs intensified. She gripped the picket fence and leaned against it for support.

The young man touched the pointed ends of the fence with his hand and let his fingers walk from picket to picket until he was directly in front of Annie Earle.

"I'm pleased to meet you, too, ma'am. But I didn't catch your name."

Annie Earle prepared to speak by sucking in a great gulp of the hot moist air. Her lips parted.

"Don't say it," commanded the young man. He extended his arm and touched Annie Earle's lips ever so lightly with the tips of his fingers. It was the slightest caress, a moth wing's brush, but it sent a wave of currents to join those in her legs. "Let me give you the name that popped into my head the moment I saw you. *Solina Angelique*. That's what came into my head when I spied you half a block away. Angel of the sun. How does that fit with you, ma'am?"

"It's awfully fancy for me," Annie Earle managed to say. "Do you go around giving everybody you meet new names?"

"Not everybody—just the people who are going to be important in my life. Doesn't Solina Angelique sound like an important name?"

"You're the strangest person I ever met, Mr. Achilles McPherson. You sure the dog days' sun hasn't affected your brain? We've had several dogs run mad this week."

Achilles shook his great shock of flame red hair and laughed. "Not yet, Solina. The sun hasn't got me yet. But if we stand here baking much longer, I might be hit by an uncontrollable seizure and take a bite out of the creamy arm of Miss Solina Angelique, which was carelessly left unguarded on the picket fence. May I have the honor of continuing this conversation with you under your mimosa tree?"

The mimosa tree stood some twenty feet down the picket fence. Achilles McPherson was on the street side of the fence. Annie Earle stood behind the fence on the yard side. *He hasn't seen my foot,* she suddenly realized. And for the first time in her life, there was someone she didn't want to know about it. It was a strange new feeling, like the tingling in her legs. *If I can work my way to the mimosa tree a little at a time and use the fence, it won't be noticeable,* she reasoned to herself. She took a couple of steps and stopped.

"I've never seen you around here before. Where are you from, Mr. McPherson?"

He stopped his progress toward the shade of the tree and turned back to answer. "I'm a traveling man. I'm from everywhere. But now I'm from here. And I'm never Mr. McPherson to the important people in my life. You may call me Achilles—he with the secret flaw in the foot—or, fair turnabout, you can give me a brand-new name."

A stab of panic shot through Annie Earle. *What did he mean by "secret flaw in the foot"?*

"What name would you give me? Come, Solina Angelique, give me a name. I dare you!"

Two more steps, even and regular, with the help of the fence.

"Let me see. What do I know about you? You're forward and brash. And you're funny and a little crazy. And you're not real. You're something that floated in on the heat of August, and you'll wash out with the relief rains that mark the end of dog days. You need a name that says all that."

Three steps with her head bent in concentration and her hand pretending to toy with the picket fence, but giving the needed support. "I reckon a good name for you would be *Billy Blue Barbarosa*."

"Would you explain that burden of a name you just hung on me?" asked Achilles McPherson.

"Well, Billy stands for someone who's real forward, like a billy goat." They both laughed. A step nearer the mimosa tree. "Blue is the silly part. Don't you think Blue is a funny name for a man?"

"I can't stop laughing," replied Achilles.

Another step. "And Barbarosa stands for all that fiery

hair leaping from your head. Pleased to meet you, Mr. Billy Blue Barbarosa."

They laughed through a couple more steps toward the pool of shade stretching from the mimosa tree. Annie Earle stopped again and leaned against the fence. "But I think I'll just call you Billy Blue, since you insist we not be formal."

Another step and the shade patch engulfed them. It sobered Annie Earle. "You still haven't told me, Mr. Achilles McPherson, who you are and where you come from."

"Well, I didn't ride in on an August heat wave, as you claim. I rode in on a tram train, owned and operated by the Great Butler Lumber Company. My pa's a logging foreman, and I'm timekeeper and payroll clerk for the company. Pa and me came down two months ago and set up bachelor quarters in the old Davies house over on Maple Street. Ma came down on the Atlantic Coast Line last week, and she's still straightening out the mess Pa and me made."

"Where do you and your folks come from?" asked Annie Earle.

My family originally comes from Virginia, up Hampton Roads way. But Pa's been following the lumber camps for more than five years, and I've been on the road with him over a year myself."

"Sounds like a mighty adventurous life you and your pa lead."

"It's got its ups and downs. But you're right, it's never dull. Always something exciting going on in a lumber camp. Every time I hear a tram train whistle moaning through the swamps, I get prickly feelings. You never know what the tram's bringing next. Now, what about you, Solina Angelique? What does an angel of the sun do for excitement around here?"

Annie Earle flushed at the sound of her new name. The way he said it almost smothered her. It was as if he were laying ownership to part of her, a strange new part of her he had just discovered and therefore maybe had some rightful claim to.

"Keeping cool is pretty much a full-time occupation around here during dog days. And for excitement we swat big, fat August flies. I'm afraid that doesn't quite come up to adventure deep in the mysterious swamps."

"Ah, how wrong you are, Solina Angelique. How wrong you are. I'd trade all the alligators and swamp moccasins for a cool glass of lemonade in one hand and a fly swatter in the other. I'm a deadly shot with a fly swatter. You should see me in action."

They both laughed. Annie Earle recovered first and said, "This is the silliest conversation I've ever had. I think you're a little crazy, Billy Blue Barbarosa."

"Then let me be completely serious." He took a step away from the fence, made a smart bow, then raised his head and leveled his steady green eyes on Annie Earle's. "May I have the honor of calling on you, Solina Angelique, that we may share the high excitement of keeping cool and swatting flies?"

Their eyes remained locked for a few seconds. Nothing was said. Annie Earle broke the tension by looking down at the picket fence that separated them.

"Would Saturday night, around eight o'clock, suit you?" asked Achilles.

Annie Earle still hesitated.

"We close down early on Saturday. It's the best night for me," added Achilles. "Could I call on you then?"

"I'll speak with my mama and let you know," Annie Earle finally replied.

"Can't you say yes right now? I'll be off to the lumber camp tomorrow and won't get back until Saturday. How will you let me know?"

Annie Earle thought quickly. "I'll send a note to your house by my friend, Queen Esther. You said your mother was home. Queen Esther can take a note to the old Davies house. I'll let you know."

"I'll be looking forward to Saturday night all week long," said Achilles. "Could I walk you back to your house now? My ma's probably already fuming because I'm late getting home for Sunday dinner. Another few minutes won't matter."

"No, thanks," said Annie Earle quickly. "It's only a step up the garden path to our house. I'll just stay for a few more minutes in this cool shade. You better be getting on to your dinner."

"I knew something special would happen to me today. Felt it first thing when I woke up this morning. Solina Angelique, you'll bring me luck. You'll see."

"You're a bit crazy, Achilles McPherson," said Annie Earle with a nervous little laugh. "You better get on home before the sun does you in."

"I'm off, but I'll be back," he said as he turned to leave. "Solina Angelique, I like the sound of that name. Solina Angelique, Solina Angelique," he chanted as he strode away.

Annie Earle watched him walk into the sun until finally he began to fade and become indistinguishable from the host of dazzle angels that returned and danced and swirled before her eyes. She began the journey down the picket fence toward the garden path—*step-slap, step-slap.* "Billy Blue," she whispered. "Oh, Billy Blue."

94

Bobo Bullard

H er sleep was charged with a sublime dream. She was running. Running. Something she'd never experienced before, even in dreams. Running, light as dandelion fluff, barely skimming the ground, keeping stride with someone by her side. They were accompanied by a host of dazzle angels, which blinded her with bursts of light like celestial fireflies. She couldn't see the face beside her, but the flaming mane of hair flickering in the flashing lights belonged to Achilles McPherson. Her body had never felt such freedom. Instead of plunging earthward with each step, she seemed to be rising just beyond the bounds of gravity. Gathering speed, he reached for her hand, and she no longer felt the earth, only the tips of grass brushing the bottoms of her bare feet. Then they soared up, up into a pure blueness, leaving the sparkling dazzle angels flickering far below.

Annie Earle woke with a start. Was that a door slamming? Or a part of the dream? A thick stillness filled the dark, warm room. She could hear her heart still pounding from the dream run. Dream run? Or an alert that something was wrong in the house? She slid out of bed and step-slapped to the window. Gray predawn mist curled and twisted through the garden below. For a moment the mists lifted near the gazebo and she saw a flash of legs dart from inside, then vanish through the privet hedge at the back of the garden. The mist closed in, and the figure was gone.

She never saw a face, or even the whole figure. But the fragment of a man, or an older boy, seen only from the shoulders down as he ran away, was sharply imprinted in her head.

With a heavy, dull ache in her foot, she dragged herself back to the bed. She sat on the edge, considering whether to wake Queen Esther and search the grounds. But it seemed silly. What could anyone want in an empty gazebo in the backyard? Nothing had ever been stolen from the Roland house. There weren't even keys to the front and back doors. Just a little night catch on the inside of the screen doors, and they weren't always snapped into place. It was probably one of the early-morning delivery boys snatching a few minutes' rest in the gazebo.

Annie Earle flipped her legs onto the bed and tried to pull back the dream. It didn't work. She fell into sound, dreamless sleep.

Aunt Charlotte was the first to notice that something was wrong. "Come look at this, Annie Earle," she called.

Annie Earle thumped out onto the back porch.

"Mighty peculiar," said Aunt Charlotte, pointing to the screen door.

"What's peculiar?'

"Look at that slit in the screen wire. Right here over the night latch."

There it was, a neat cut about a hand's width into the screen.

"Did you put the latch on last night?" asked Annie Earle.

"Sure did. And it was off this morning. I just noticed that cut in the screen wire."

Annie Earle started to mention what she had seen last night but decided not to.

"Looks like somebody tried to break into the house. You notice anything missing, Aunt Charlotte?"

"Well, it ain't occurred to me to look till right now. Queen Esther! Come here, Queen," she called. "We better look through the whole house. This is peculiar. I don't like it."

They searched the downstairs and found nothing missing or disturbed.

"We'd better do the upstairs, too," said Aunt Charlotte. "Though I hate to even think that somebody might of gone upstairs without any of us hearing a sound."

They left Mama's room to the last, since she was still sleeping. None of the other rooms revealed any signs of an intruder.

"You think we ought to bother Miss Nel?" asked Aunt Charlotte.

"Why don't you go bring up some coffee for her. That way it won't look like we're coming in for a search," Annie Earle suggested.

"Coffee's already made. I'll be right back," said Aunt Charlotte.

Annie Earle drew Queen aside as soon as Aunt Charlotte was down the stairs.

"Queen, there was somebody in the house last night," she whispered.

"You see somebody?"

"Not in the house. I heard a door slam. I was dreaming and I woke up. I wasn't sure the noise I heard wasn't part of my dream. So I went over to the window and looked out. The yard was boiling with fog and mist, but I saw somebody run out from the gazebo."

"Somebody you know?"

"I can't be sure. I didn't see his face. Or even his whole body. I just saw him from the shoulders down."

"Dog days be dangerous times," muttered Queen Esther.

Aunt Charlotte returned with the coffee, and they went into Mama's room.

"Miss Nel, wake up," called Aunt Charlotte. "Time for your morning lift. Louisiana coffee laced with chicory. Here, let me put a pillow to your back."

Queen Esther raised the blinds while Annie Earle searched the room with her eyes.

Mama sat up, rubbed her eyelids, and smoothed her hair with her hands. "Hand me my bed jacket, Annie Earle," she said. "I never could break my morning fast without getting dressed for it. Just because one has to stay in bed is no reason not to keep up standards."

Annie Earle held the jacket while Mama slipped her arms through the lacy half sleeves. "Now give me my earrings. I never feel really dressed without them. Would you hand them to me, Queen Esther? They're right there on the dresser where I left them last night."

Queen searched the dresser for the earrings. "You sure you left them on the dresser, Miss Nel? I don't see them here. Maybe they on the night table."

"No. They're on the dresser. I'm sure I left them there. I remember just before I went to bed, I was looking at them in the mirror, admiring the lovely design. Mr. Roland gave them to me before we were married. Don't you think pearls and amethyst complement each other? They're right there on the dresser beside my purse. That's where I left them, right beside the purse."

"Miss Nel, they's no purse here, either," said Queen Esther.

"Well, that's mighty peculiar," said Mama.

"We'll find them. They've got to be here somewhere," said Annie Earle quickly.

But a thorough search of the room turned up neither purse nor earrings.

Finally Annie Earle said, "Mama, there's something we have to tell you. Somebody broke into the house last night. Whoever it was cut the back door screen and lifted the night latch."

"Annie Earle, that's hard to believe. Never have I had the slightest fear of being robbed by colored or white."

"Well, Mama, it looks like it's happened. I think we have to call in the police."

"Police in my house? Oh, Annie Earle, I never thought—"

"Mama, what was in your purse?"

"Well, I always like to be prepared, just in case."

"What was in the purse, Mama?"

"Twenty dollars and some change. All these years, there's never been the slightest problem."

"Wait till Aunt Kat gets a whiff of this. Oh, Mama!"

"Do we have to call in the police?" asked Mama.

"I'm going right now," said Annie Earle. "We can't pretend this didn't happen. Queen Esther, where's Brodie? I'd forgotten all about him with all this going on."

"Brodie's downstairs having breakfast. I sent him to the kitchen so I could search his room."

"Don't mention this to him yet. I'll figure out how to tell him when I get back from the police."

The police station was a small wooden building with a front porch flush with the street. Annie Earle pulled up the two squeaky steps to the plank porch and step-slapped her way into the station. Officer Tolbert Bullard was on duty.

Annie Earle knew the officer by sight, but never recalled having spoken directly to him. She remembered vaguely that he was the uncle of that hateful Bobo she almost choked to death in Cattail Bay. She was very self-conscious about entering the station. Women rarely went inside, especially white women.

For a moment Annie Earle was about to turn around and leave. It had suddenly occurred to her that she could ask Jack Cato to do this. But Officer Bullard was asking her something.

"I was saying, Miss Roland, what could we do for you."

"We've been robbed, Mr. Tolbert," she blurted out.

"Robbed? How's that, Miss Roland?"

"Somebody came in the house last night and took Mama's pocketbook and earrings."

"That sounds serious, Miss Roland. I think I'd better come right over."

"No, sir, wait till I get back and get Mama ready. She's upset right now. I'd appreciate it if you'd come over in about an hour."

"That'll be fine, Miss Roland. There's some preliminary inquiries I can put out in the meantime. Tell your mama I'll be over in an hour."

When Officer Bullard arrived, he brought the county deputy sheriff, Mr. Davies, with him. Annie Earle and Mama had agreed that no one was to mention the amount of money in the pocketbook. Annie Earle decided to tell the officers about the figure she had seen running from the gazebo. But her description was such a fragment, the officers admitted it didn't give them much to go on. They took down the skimpy facts and promised to get to the bottom of the mystery right away.

"This is a small, tight little town, Miss Penelope," said Officer Bullard. "Not much can happen we don't zero in on before too long. I wager we'll have the culprit and your belongings before the week is up."

Mama thanked them and said she certainly hoped so. Then she asked Officer Bullard, "Mr. Tolbert, do you think we ought to have keys made for the front and back doors?"

"It's a shame to admit it, but I reckon you should," he replied.

For two days nothing happened. No word from Officer Bullard. And no word from Aunt Kat. The whole town had the story, so Annie Earle knew there was no way Aunt Kat didn't know.

Then on Wednesday morning everything exploded. The postman brought a registered letter, addressed to Mrs. Penelope Roland. Annie Earle signed for it and rushed up to Mama's room.

"It's from the clerk of the county court," said Annie Earle. "I can tell from the return address."

"It's Katherine. I know it," cried Mama. "Open it. Read it to me."

Annie Earle ripped open the envelope and flipped out the official-looking stationery.

"It's a summons, Mama. Aunt Kat's demanding a hearing to determine your competency. It's filed through those Powell lawyers."

"Not being surprised still doesn't make me prepared for this. Katherine's my sister, but she's an evil woman, cloaking herself in the name of the Lord."

Annie Earle extended the summons toward Mama.

"Take it to Jack Cato. I won't touch the thing. Get it out of my sight. And get me my pills before you leave."

Annie Earle headed toward the kitchen to tell Aunt Charlotte that she was going to see Jack Cato. Before she reached the kitchen, she heard Queen Esther's voice, high-pitched and excited.

"It's so, Gramma Charlotte. It's so! They've got him locked up already."

"Got who locked up?" asked Annie Earle as she entered the room.

"Kitty Fisher. They locked him up this morning. They claiming he stole Miss Nel's earrings and pocketbook. They got a witness say he saw Kitty leaving the house. They got Kitty's cap. Say he lost it in the hedge in the backyard. They got Kitty framed good!"

"Hold on, Queen. Who says they saw Kitty Fisher?"

"Bobo Bullard. That lying, good-for-nothing Bobo."

Bobo's threat in Cattail Bay echoed in Annie Earle's head, *"I'll get you, you and your nigger friend, Old Crooked Foot!"*

"Kitty's mama been down to the jail. Kitty say he lost his hat last Saturday at the icehouse. Bobo was working there over the weekend. Kitty swear he ain't come near this place on Sunday night. And his mama say he be sleeping till she wake him up late on Monday morning."

"Hush, Queen, let me think. Kitty's in big trouble. I don't believe for a second he robbed our house," said Annie Earle.

"If it be Kitty's word against Bobo, you know who they gonna believe. Kitty won't stand a chance in court," wailed Queen Esther.

"Queen, settle down. I've got to think. But first I've got to go down to Jack Cato's office. Aunt Kat's started legal proceedings to have Mama declared incompetent."

On the way to Jack Cato's office, Annie Earle crossed the street to keep from passing in front of the police station. She was glad she'd made the detour, for even from the opposite side of the wide street she could see Bobo lounging on the porch. His thumbs were hooked under red suspenders that he kept snapping against his chest. She wasn't ready to face him yet.

"I guess I made the mistake of thinking Bobo was all talk and dumber than he is," she muttered to herself.

Jack Cato received the news with an exasperated sigh. "Well, that's a double header we have here."

"You've got to get Kitty Fisher out of this."

"First things first, Miss Roland. I can get a postponement of this hearing on the grounds that your mama's not physically well enough right now. That'll put a stay on Miss Katherine for a while. This Kitty Fisher business is trickier."

"What do they usually do in a case like Kitty's?"

"If it goes to court, and with that cap evidence it probably will, a chain gang sentence for Kitty Fisher is a sure bet."

"That Bobo's lying. I just know it!"

"Now, calm down," said Jack Cato, taking her gently by the arm. He led her toward the door. "I don't like seeing you so upset. Go on back home and let me think of a way we can come up with some hard evidence to prove what you think you *just know*!"

The floorboards under her worry rocker were creaking at a fast, irritating clip.

Slow it down, Annie Earle. Slow it down. Think back over everything that happened Sunday night. The running dream. Achilles McPherson, the traveling man. The door slamming. The mist in the backyard. That fleeting piece of a person running from the gazebo. Heavy work shoes, blue pants. God, I wish the fog had lifted so I could have seen his face. Oh, cripes, how can you identify somebody from the shoulders down? Everybody around here wears work shoes and dark blue pants.

Wait a minute. Yes, Annie Earle, you've been missing something. There were red suspenders holding up those dark blue pants. Red suspenders—just like the ones Bobo was snapping against his chest at the police station. Jack Cato, we've got it! Here's your hard evidence. It wasn't Kitty. It was that stinking Bobo!

She braced her strong foot against the floor, stopping the rocker. The good feeling of resolving part of a difficult problem settled over her. But it lasted only a few moments. She began rocking again.

Wait a minute. Going to Jack Cato won't do. It'll be my word against Bobo's. I've got to do this myself. Yes, Annie Earle, you've got to face Bobo all alone. There's got to be a way to bring that bully around.

She pushed out of the chair and called, "Queen Esther, where are you?"

"Here in the kitchen," answered Queen.

"Will you come out to the porch? I need your help on two important matters."

Queen Esther popped out onto the porch, drying her hands on her apron. "What kind of matters?" she asked.

"One you won't like. So let's settle that one first."

"What won't I like?"

"You've got to deliver a note for me to Bobo over at the ice house."

"You're right. I don't like that one a bit. What's the other one?"

"Help me pick out a dress to wear Saturday night when Achilles McPherson comes to sit."

"That I be pleased to do."

"You don't think this one could be a shiner like that Tommy Hickman, do you?" asked Annie Earle.

"Can't tell yet what kind of fish this Achilles man be. But I got a feeling this one ain't no shiner."

The Sitting

$\cdots\!\bullet\!\!-\!\!\blacktriangleright\!\!\blacklozenge\!\!\blacktriangleright\!\!-\!\!\bullet\!\cdots$

He strode in at dusk through the haze of a threatening cloudburst, a pale phantom with shocking red hair. Light, milky ground fog rising from the steamy gravel of the garden path swirled around his feet, giving him the appearance of floating. From her sheltered seat on the porch behind the Virginia creeper vines, Annie Earle watched the white-clad figure change from a ghost to the reality of Achilles McPherson in a stiffly starched summer suit. He took the steps two at a time, and with a couple of long strides reached the front door and raised his hand to rattle the bell chime.

"Evening, Achilles McPherson," said Annie Earle softly.

Achilles turned with a start at the sound of his name coming from the vine-draped part of the porch. With his hand still raised he peered hard at the figure half-hidden in the deep shadows.

"Won't you pull up a chair and join me here in the cool?"

"Solina Angelique! You gave me a start. Such a start. A few more sudden surprises like that and I'll have to rename you—something that stands for a dark, mysterious lady of the shadows."

He pulled a rocker next to Annie Earle's chair and sat down. "It is cool here. I half expected your mother to answer the door and usher me into a hot, stuffy parlor where we'd all sit and make polite talk while I'd be worried whether I'm sweating right through my pants. This is nice. Real nice."

"Mama's not feeling well. This weather's just laid her low. We had some things stolen from the house this week. Nothing of value really. But it shook Mama up, all the same. She sends her regards and says she's sorry to miss meeting a young man with a name like Billy Blue Barbarosa."

As Annie Earle heard her own laughter mingle with that of the young man, the real scene she had played with Mama rushed through her mind again.

Queen Esther said, "What's the point in asking Miss Nel about this man? She won't know what you're talking about. Just write that note and I'll run it over to the old Davies house. You ain't been asking Miss Nel about nothing important lately. Why you bothering her about this?"

"I want to ask her. I never had a chance before. You coming up with me? I see you got towels for Mama's room."

"I'm looking through you, Annie Earle. I'm looking right through you. What you scared about?"

Annie Earle began pulling up the staircase. "Scared? I don't know where you come up with things, Queen Esther. You're just plain superstitious. What in the world would I be scared about?"

"I ain't superstitious, but I can read signs. I ain't figured it out yet. Maybe you scared of tall, good-looking, strange men," said Queen, scampering ahead on the staircase.

Annie Earle attempted to swat her on the fanny, but Queen Esther was too fast. From the top of the staircase, Queen turned and looked back. "I'm getting a bead on it now," said Queen Esther under her breath. "Yeah, I see it now. You fooling this Billy Blue man, and you scared. I don't know yet what you fooling him about, but it's got you scared, Annie Earle. You might as well tell me. I'll get it, anyway."

"Stop it, Queen. I don't like it. I'm not scared, and you're talking foolishness."

Annie Earle and Queen Esther entered Mama's room. The frail figure propped on a mountain of pillows with long, dark curly hair framing a childlike face could pass for a young woman in the shaded room. Aunt Charlotte indulged herself in the care of Mama's hair, and it responded in luxuriant growth. She often said as she combed and brushed the dark tresses, "If only I had such luck with the rest of you, Miss Nel."

"Mama," Annie Earle called gently, "Mama, open your eyes. I've got something I want to talk to you about."

The pale face stirred. Queen Esther busied herself with the towels at a chifforobe. Annie Earle touched Mama's hair with the tips of her fingers. "Mama?"

"No, not now, Annie Earle. I'm not up to talking about the robbery. It's better not to think about. I never thought Kitty Fisher—"

"Mama, listen. I'm not here to worry you about that. Mama, a young man has asked to call on me. He's new in town and works for the Great Butler Lumber Company. I told him I'd have to ask you before I gave my answer. Do you hear me, Mama?"

"Yes, I hear. I hear. Your father, Mr. Roland, was a lumberman. Is this young man Irish?"

"I don't know, Mama. But if red hair and the gift of gab mean anything, he's Irish, all right."

"Sounds like Mr. Roland. Child, child, you don't have

any choice. Irish men are fey and determined, and once they've cast an eye on you, you don't have any choice. Oh, I hope he's kind, baby. Oh, Lord, I hope he's kind and gentle."

"Mama, he's only asked to sit with me this Saturday night. That's all."

"All. All. That's right. They want everything. And they get it, too. They take all of you and make it just a little corner of them, and then they up and die and carry with them the part of you they've taken away. They leave you hollow and empty and lonely and helpless and sad, and I need my medicine."

Annie Earle quickly shook two pills into Mama's trembling hand. Dr. Whittaker had removed the four-a-day instruction from the bottle recently. It simply read, "Take two tablets when needed."

Queen Esther poured a glass of water and held it to Mama's mouth. She whispered to Annie Earle, "What are you hiding?"

Annie Earle ignored the question. "So, Mama, I wanted to get your permission to allow this young man to call on me."

"It's written in the book. I've got no more choice in the matter. And no more strength to fight it. Yes, Mr. Roland, you may call on me and you may end up having your way with me."

Mama paused. Annie Earle and Queen Esther exchanged looks.

"Pity of it was, I loved him. Pity he had that stroke. Pity the amethyst earrings he gave me got stolen. Pity, pity, pity . . ." Mama's voice trailed off, and she twisted her face into the pillows.

"I'm afraid I've set her off," said Annie Earle. "There,

Mama, it's all right. Let me shift your pillows. That'll make you feel better. There, now, Queen Esther and I'll stop bothering you so your pills can take effect."

As they walked down the staircase, Queen Esther spoke quietly. "I figured out what you're hiding from that young man. You don't have to tell me."

Not yet, Annie Earle pleaded with herself. *Not just yet. Give yourself a little more time.*

To Achilles McPherson she said, "Tell me, what's it like in a lumber camp? I've heard all kinds of things go on way back in the swamp."

"Most camps pretty much live up to their reputations. You usually get a wild bunch living there. There's a lot of drinking and a fair amount of fighting. In a way each camp is a little town, but without all the rules and regulations that keep a regular community in line."

"Do most of the workers live right in the camps?" asked Annie Earle.

"Yeah, most everybody lives in the camp during the week. The locals come home on the weekends, but a lot of them live in the swamp all the time. Some have their wives there, too."

"I've heard there are other women who live in the camps," remarked Annie Earle.

"Yeah, you heard right. There's always a few women, taking in washing and things. They can cause a lot of trouble in a camp. Pa says if it was up to him, he'd never let a woman under fifty set foot in a lumber camp."

"Too bad. I was just going to say how much I'd like to see a lumber camp. Sounds like a mighty interesting place."

"It's not all fighting and carrying on. Most of the time

it's pretty nice. Especially after supper, when the guitar players and the banjo pickers gather round a big campfire and play and sing. And there's buck dancing the likes of which you've never seen. The men challenge each other with different steps, and each one tries to outdo the other. Do you like dancing?"

Annie Earle was startled by the question. "Sure, sure."

"I'm nuts about dancing. Wish I could cut a step like those colored men at the camp."

"Oh, I'd sure like to see one of those singing and dancing affairs," said Annie Earle wistfully. "But good gracious, I'm just sitting here fascinated by what goes on in those lumber camps and neglecting to offer you a cool drink of lemonade. You must be as dry as August fodder from all this heat."

"That offer does have a refreshing sound to it."

Time's up, Annie Earle, she told herself. *Let him know. Let him see.* She stood up and took one step away from the chair. Suddenly the Virginia creeper vines rustled and parted just above the porch boards. A pale face surrounded by white curls peered through the dark, leafy opening.

"Brodie!" gasped Annie Earle. "You scared me half to death! Get out of that vine and come in the house."

Achilles was on his feet, staring speechless at the apparition in the vines.

"I lost my giant night moth. Had my hand right on him, but he got away," said Brodie.

"This ghost you see here is my brother. I mean this face you see here in the vines belongs to my brother, Brodie Lacewell," explained Annie Earle. "He collects butterflies and moths and all kinds of flying things. And he usually doesn't go around scaring people half to death."

Achilles made a quick recovery. "Well, I'm more than relieved to learn that you're not a ghost, Brodie Lacewell, and very pleased to meet you." He bent down and thrust a hand into the vines, and he and Brodie shook somewhere in the tangle of leaves.

"Come on up on the porch and have some lemonade with us," said Annie Earle as she started to move again. *Step-slap, step-slap.* Rocking deep to the right side, she passed in front of Achilles McPherson and disappeared through the front door. She had not looked at him in passing, and she resisted pausing at the front door to look back.

Once in the hall, she said with the slightest whisper, "Now he knows, Annie Earle. Now he knows, and he may be gone when I get back with the lemonade. In all my life I've never fooled anybody about my condition before, and I never before hated myself for having it. What's happening to me? What's happening?"

Annie Earle was startled to hear a voice reply, "You learning to fly, honey. I do believe you ready to spread your wings."

"Queen Esther! You've finished me off! Brodie just scared the living daylights out of me, now you. Whatever are you doing lurking behind this staircase?"

"Passing from the kitchen to Miss Nel's room ain't exactly lurking. I'm sorry if I scared you, but you stared right past me and you were mumbling to yourself."

"I'm sorry, Queen, but I'm so nervous, I'm shaky."

"Nervous birds can't fly too well. You got to lift up light and easy and just let yourself rise. Flying means getting outside yourself. Being a little scared is all right, but nervous just drags you down."

"Queen, you're talking to Annie Earle, not some bird."

"There's some bird in everybody. Pity is, most folks never learns about it. You're wanting to fly bad, Annie Earle. I can just feel your wings trembling to try."

"I can't stand here listening to this crazy talk with my guest dying of thirst on the front porch."

Queen Esther moved lightly up the staircase. Annie Earle pushed on into the kitchen. *Step-slap, step-slap.* She plodded back to the front porch, carefully balancing the tray with glasses and a sweating pitcher of tinkling ice and lemonade.

He was still there, and he was talking with Brodie Lacewell. And what was more amazing to Annie Earle, Brodie Lacewell was talking to him. Brodie, who never spoke to strangers, was explaining to this one about giant night moths. Some of the heaviness that pervaded Annie Earle's return trip from the kitchen suddenly lifted. She felt it, just like Queen said, rising, rising, and floating away outside herself.

"Could I interrupt you gentlemen by offering you something to drink?"

"You sure could," answered Achilles. "You know your brother must have the biggest collection of local flying life I've ever heard of. He's been telling me about it. I'm eager to see that collection."

"Well, he's been doing it since he was knee-high to a butterfly," said Annie Earle.

"Achilles was telling me about some strange-colored butterflies that flit around hibiscus flowers deep in the swamp near the lumber camp," said Brodie. "I'd sure like to have one of those purple ones with the swallowtails for my collection."

"Well, Brodie, I'd be more than delighted to bring one back for you, if ever I get an invitation to visit a lumber camp," answered Annie Earle. She handed Achilles a tall glass of lemonade.

"You're turning this business about visiting a lumber camp into a challenge for me, aren't you?"

"Well, it does seem to me that you keep implying that nice girls wouldn't be caught dead in a lumber camp. I guess there's too much excitement there for nice girls to handle. But I tell you fair, Mr. Billy Blue Barbarosa, I'm a nice girl and I'm dying to see what goes on in those camps."

"And I answer you fair, Solina Angelique, two weeks from tomorrow, I'd be pleased to take you to the Great Butler Lumber Camp in the heart of the Green Swamp, where alligators outnumber men and contests will be held for banjo picking and buck dancing. Now the challenge is yours. Well, Solina Angelique, what's your answer?"

"Two weeks from Sunday next is fine, Billy Blue, just fine."

Achilles and Annie Earle drifted into the pleasantries of small talk, while Brodie dozed. It was late when Annie Earle noticed the eerie shadows the moon was casting through the creeper vines. "That murky moon is circled with rain rings," she said. "But I doubt we'll get any before dog days are over."

"It's late, and I must catch the tram train at daybreak," said Achilles McPherson.

"I'll walk you to the garden gate," said Annie Earle.

He took her arm on her right and vulnerable side, and they began the trip. As they went down the steps, Brodie Lacewell roused and called after them, "You won't forget the purple butterfly with the black swallowtails?"

"On my life, I promise we'll bring it back for you," answered Annie Earle.

Step-slap, step-slap. She rocked against Achilles' strong arm as they proceeded down the garden path. At the gate she said, "Good-night, Billy Blue."

He pressed her hand and said, "There's a big empty weekend between now and our trip to the lumber camp. May I sit with you again next Saturday?"

"Why, yes. Yes, that would be nice."

He answered, "Saturday next, Solina Angelique." And the sound of her new name lingered in the air, circling her head like the rustle of bird wings.

The Bribe

---◆--▶---◆---

In her stockings she slid her right foot forward along the floor, then brought her strong left foot up to it. It was her secret way of walking so as not to make the step-slap sound. Silently she entered Mama's room and moved to the tall chifforobe. *Bottom drawer. Easy. Dear God, don't let it squeak.* Her hand felt under the cool silk nightgowns and found the smooth lacquered box.

She pulled the box from the drawer, turned toward the bed, and listened. Mama's deep, pill-induced breathing pulsed through the room. Reassured, she ran her finger over the *mille fleur*-patterned box, seeking the tiny yellow flower with the orange center. She pressed it and the lid rose, revealing a stack of crisp green bills. She stuffed a handful into her pocket, then squeezed the box lid tightly, making a sharp clicking sound as the lock snapped into place.

Mama stirred. Annie Earle held her breath and the box, both suspended until Mama's regular breathing settled in again. She eased from the room.

Stealing from my own mother. On a Sunday morning. What would Aunt Kat make of that? Dear Mama, what will you make of it? It's not true stealing, Mama. You always said, "That's our emergency fund, Annie Earle. The money's put aside for the unexpected that needs to be handled without anyone knowing." Well, Mama, this is one of those times. Settling with Bobo sure fits your definition.

She was to meet him in the backyard gazebo at a little

past eleven o'clock. It was the best time and place she could think of. Aunt Charlotte and Queen Esther would be at church. Mama's windows faced the front of the house. Brodie always spent Sunday morning with his mail-order catalogs that offered science experiment paraphernalia. It was better and safer than the isolated fairgrounds that she had first considered. Her greatest fear was that he wouldn't come near the spot where he'd committed the crime he'd pinned on Kitty Fisher. She was counting a lot on Bobo's greed.

When he pushed through the thick hedges in the backyard, she was relieved and frightened at the same time. Close up Bobo looked bigger and tougher than she remembered. He sidled over to the gazebo and stood looking down at her, thumbs hooked under red suspenders.

"Nigger girl brought me a note down at the icehouse," he said.

"Queen Esther took you the note," replied Annie Earle, hating the way he said "nigger" when referring to Queen.

"She know what's in that note?"

"No."

"Just you and me, huh?" asked Bobo.

"Just us."

"Well, what did you mean by 'There's lots more where this came from if you want to play ball'?"

"Just that, Bobo. That ten dollars in the note was a down payment."

"What kind of down payment?"

"The down payment for a little change in your story about Kitty Fisher's cap."

Bobo took a step back and looked furtively over his shoulder. The backyard was still and quiet with the

Sunday church hour pall that hung over the whole of Vineland.

"That nigger done it. What's it to you? Uncle Tolbert's gonna get him a chain gang sentence. That ought to make your mama real glad."

That was just the response Annie Earle expected from Bobo. It was time to put her hunch to the test.

"Bobo, how would you like to come by a quick two hundred dollars, real fast?"

"I thought we was talking about sending a nigger to the chain gang."

"Well, that might give you some satisfaction, Bobo, but you can't spend satisfaction."

"Two hundred dollars, you said?"

"Yes. Cash."

"You'd pay two hundred dollars to get that nigger off? He must be servicing you and that Queen Esther both. I never—"

"Bobo! Cut your dirty-mouth business!" *Oh, my God, I've flubbed it. He won't be bought off!*

She grabbed his arm, surprising him with the strength of her grip. He wrenched free, probably remembering those same strong hands around his throat in Cattail Bay.

"How you want me to change my story?" he stammered.

Annie Earle sat down on the gazebo bench. Maybe there was still a chance. "You got it a little mixed up, Bobo," she began. "You were mistaken about where you found Kitty Fisher's cap. It was really at the icehouse. Not in that hedge in our backyard. That's all. Just straighten out your story."

"My uncle will kill me if I do that. If I say I found the cap at the icehouse, he ain't got no case."

"And you ain't got no two hundred dollars, Bobo, if

you don't tell the truth about where you found that cap."

"He'll kill me. Two hundred dollars! Take forever to get that much ahead."

Annie Earle pulled the bills from her pocket. "It would take you about two minutes to straighten out your story with Officer Bullard. Then this is yours, Bobo. All yours. Except for one other little thing." She stuffed the money back into her pocket.

"What little thing?"

"I want Mama's earrings back."

Bobo turned his back on Annie Earle. "I ain't admitting that I got them earrings."

"You don't have to admit anything, Bobo. Just return them. Let's say there'll be an extra twenty dollars for the person who finds Mama's earrings. We'll leave it that way."

"You think you got it all figured out. You think you can dangle some money in front of me and get me to save your nigger friend. I don't understand you one bit. If we whites don't stick together, every nigger in this town will start getting out of line."

He turned toward Annie Earle. His face was twisted, and his mouth trembled at the corners. He looked like he might cry. "That would be two hundred and twenty dollars in all?" he asked.

"Two hundred and twenty," repeated Annie Earle. She fought back the urge to feel sorry for the crumbling bully who was on the verge of tears in his struggle with greed and prejudice.

"I'll let you know," he said, turning to leave.

"Wait! Right now, Bobo. Right now, or our deal's off. And I go down to the police station and swear I saw you run out of the house the night of the robbery. I did, Bobo. It was your red suspenders that gave you away. I did see you. It would make a messy case in court, Bobo. I'd do it in a minute. But Mama won't want that. And I don't want to put any more pressures on Mama. It's clean and neat this way. Besides, if you make me go the messy way, you don't get a penny, Bobo."

A tear dribbled down his cheek as he choked out, "You win again, Old Crooked Foot. But this time I get something, too."

At the words *crooked foot* she smothered the surprising sympathy she was starting to feel for Bobo. "Do it first thing tomorrow morning, Bobo. I don't want this to drag out any longer. Then meet me right here tomorrow night for your money."

"All right, all right," he mumbled, rubbing his fist against his nose. As he slunk back through the privet hedge, she heard him mutter, "Uncle Tolbert's gonna kill me."

She returned to the still, hushed house, feeling shaky but relieved to have the meeting with Bobo over. Her hand toyed with the bills in her pocket. She didn't dare return them to Mama's room. Besides, she'd need them tomorrow night, anyway. Where should she hide them? The dragon cachepot in the parlor, under the dried rose petals, next to Granny Buzzard's conjure bag.

When she slipped the bills into the pot, her fingers touched the conjure bag. It yielded to the touch like a soft, live thing. She yanked her hand from the pot, knocking it onto its side. Rose petals spilled out on the table like bloodstained snowflakes. "That thing gives me the heebie-jeebies!" she muttered. "I still don't believe in it, but it does make my skin crawl."

She scooped up the petals, sifted them back into the cachepot, and closed the lid.

· · ·

Monday was a day of darting and dodging and pretend business, punctuated by fleeting thoughts of Achilles McPherson. He certainly didn't appear to be a shiner. All day Annie Earle steered clear of Queen Esther, afraid Queen would look right through her and divine the whole Bobo business. She wasn't sure why she didn't want Queen to know. Something told her she'd better keep it a secret from everyone. Otherwise it could backfire.

At suppertime she was trapped with Brodie, Aunt Charlotte, and Queen Esther, all sharing the evening meal.

"All day you been acting like a dog just hid a bone," said Queen Esther.

"What does that mean?" asked Annie Earle.

"Means that it's plain as day you got secrets."

"I love secrets. Tell us a secret," begged Brodie Lacewell.

"It wouldn't be a secret if I told, now, would it, Brodie?"

"I guess not," said Brodie.

Queen Esther sniffed, shook her shoulders, and said in a singsong voice.

> *"A secret, a secret,*
> *Hallelujah, Amen!*
> *Hide it from your foes,*
> *But share it with your friends!"*

"Come on, Annie Earle, share, share!" chorused Aunt Charlotte and Brodie Lacewell.

She wanted to tell them about Bobo. This was the small family circle that would close around her, keeping her secrets secret as long as they needed to be kept. But she held back, fearing that to tell might jeopardize the

120

whole plan. She attempted to answer back in Queen's style.

> *"Oh, yes, I have a secret,*
> *Hallelujah, Amen!*
> *It will hold until tomorrow*
> *And I'll tell you then!"*

They all laughed at her reply. Aunt Charlotte moved from the table to pour more coffee. Suddenly Queen Esther's face was grave, her mouth tight, and her eyes narrowed on Annie Earle.

Annie Earle had the strange sensation that Queen was eavesdropping on her thoughts. "It's going to work out all right with Kitty Fisher," she said quietly to Queen.

"It's got to do with your secret," replied Queen, frowning.

"Mr. Cato's going to take care of everything," said Annie Earle, trying to steer Queen away.

Aunt Charlotte returned to the table with coffee and fresh-picked huckleberries, topped with whipped cream.

"Who's ready for my blue gum special?" she asked.

"Me!" "Me!" "Me!" everyone shouted. Aunt Charlotte chuckled as she passed out the berries. "Hold it," she cried. "No whipped cream for Miss Annie Earle."

Despite hints of secrets and everyone's piqued curiosity, Annie Earle still managed to slip out of the house and to the gazebo without being seen. The bribe money in her pocket seemed to throb against her thigh. Had it taken on life from Granny Buzzard's conjure bag? Alone in the dark, she began to catalog her fears.

What if Bobo doesn't show up?

What if he'd rather see Kitty on the chain gang than pocket more money than he'd ever come by working for it?

What if Aunt Kat gets wind of this? It would surely strike her as evidence that Mama is incapable of managing her affairs and we're just sitting ducks, waiting for foxes like Bobo to pick us off.

What if Kitty goes to the chain gang? I don't think I could ever look Queen Esther in the face again, should that come about.

What if—

He burst through the privet hedge and scooted to the gazebo. "I done it," he said. "I done it. Now I want my money."

He looked big and mean again.

"I'm glad to hear that, Bobo. Tell me exactly what you've done."

"Told Uncle Tolbert I was wrong about where I found Kitty Fisher's cap. Thought he was gonna bust me right in the mouth. But he didn't. He just looked at me and said, 'You're a disappointment, Bobo. I thought you had the makings of a policeman. Thought you understood how things ought to be handled in this town. Must be that weak blood on your mother's side coming through.' Well, when he said that about my ma, I stood up to him and told him plain out, 'You better let that nigger go, 'cause you ain't got no case, Uncle Tolbert.'"

"And what did Officer Bullard say?"

"He said the nigger would be out tomorrow morning, and he'd reopen the case. That bothers me."

"Don't worry, Bobo. The case will be closed as soon as Kitty Fisher's out. I intend to inform Mr. Bullard that we've found Mama's earrings and pocketbook and we're sorry to have put him to such trouble."

"What about my money?"

"The earrings, Bobo?"

"Yeah, right here." He thrust his hands into his pocket and fished out the pearl-and-amethyst earrings.

122

Annie Earle dug into her pocket for the bills. They felt charged to her hands. As she passed them to Bobo, she heard Queen Esther sounding a warning call.

"Annie Earle! Where are you, Annie Earle? Miss Kat's here!" Queen came down the back steps with a lantern in her hand.

The screen door on the back porch slammed. Aunt Kat plunged down the steps.

"Annie Earle? There you are! Nel's talking pure nonsense."

At the sound of the voices, Bobo jammed the money into his pocket and ran from the gazebo.

"Who's that darting through those hedges?" shouted Aunt Kat. "I could take oath it looked like that no-good Bobo Bullard. What's going on here? This is a mad-house!"

Annie Earle stepped from the gazebo.

"Aunt Kat, what in the world are you doing here?"

"What am I doing? Fine question. What are *you* doing, miss? Cavorting in the gazebo with white trash?"

"You're jumping to conclusions, Aunt Kat."

"Our family name means nothing to you. I can see that clearly now."

"You're wrong, Aunt Kat. My family means a lot to me. That's why I won't let you or anybody else break it up. Now, what did you want from Mama?"

"Well, you're certainly changing from a sweet, afflicted child to a disrespectful wench. It seems I can't hold a civil conversation with anybody in this family. I just dropped by on a sisterly visit to say that I will not be put off by these legal dodges that weasel Jack Cato is pulling with his delays."

"Mama's not up to a court hearing right now. You know that."

"I wanted to check for myself. Nel has her tricks. And I'm sure she's pulling one right now, pretending to be worse off than she is. She talked nothing but nonsense when I tried to discuss this messy robbery business with her."

Annie Earle step-slapped past Aunt Kat. "I'd better go check on Mama," she said.

"You may walk away from me now, miss, but I'm a patient one. I'll bide my time."

Annie Earle pulled herself up the back steps onto the porch. She snapped the new night latch on the screen door.

"Good-night, Aunt Kat."

Queen Esther walked silently with her into the house. When they were safely inside she asked, "You ready to share your secret yet?"

"I said tomorrow. But I'm bursting to tell you right now. Kitty Fisher'll be out of jail tomorrow."

Queen Esther hugged her tightly.

Night Scare

Jack Cato said he didn't understand it at all. Kitty Fisher released, and no charges brought against him. "It doesn't make sense. Doesn't fit the character of the Officer Bullard I know. Sure puzzles me the way it's turned out. Hard to believe," he concluded, shaking his head.

Annie Earle smiled and said, "I'm beginning to believe in the strangest things. Doesn't surprise me that much."

Jack Cato gave her a piercing eye search, the kind that made her think, *This smart cat smells that I'm not telling him everything I know.* But he surprised her with his response. "I've got the legal order delaying Miss Penelope's appearance to determine her competency until Dr. Whittaker certifies that she's fit to appear personally in court. For the time being, that'll keep Miss Katherine chafing at the bit, but on a short leash, or, better still, on a choke chain."

Aunt Kat on a choke chain with the leash held by Jack Cat. Lord, I'm going to slip up and call him Cat for sure—that's the funniest thing I can imagine, or ever hope for.

She exploded in a fit of giggles, and soon Jack Cato, too, was laughing out of control. Jack recovered first. "Well," he said, "from this time on, since informality has invaded our relationship, may I call you Annie Earle rather than Miss Roland?"

Annie Earle subdued her giggles, nodded, and stopped short of asking if, in return, she could call him Jack Cat.

His next statement sobered her and took her completely by surprise. "Would you consider it forward, Annie Earle, if I asked to come to sit with you this Saturday night?"

He was asking her for a date. Too many scrambled thoughts tumbled through her head, all in a confused jumble. *Is he after the Roland money? How old is he, anyway? Twenty-three or -four, maybe? Is he sincere? Does he really like me? I've gone through all of high school in Vineland, and no one in this town has ever hinted at a date. Achilles McPherson is different. Sun gods don't grow in Vineland soil. And shiners like Tommy Hickman don't count.*

The long silence was embarrassing for her. "I'm flattered, Jack," she finally managed. "But this Saturday, I'm engaged."

"I see," he replied. "I hope I didn't overstep my bounds."

"No. No, not at all," she said. "I'll be going along now."

He pounced from the chair to the door to see her out.

He does move like a cat. A pretty graceful cat, I'd say. No sun god. But there is something nice about him.

Annie Earle walked home feeling light and airy despite the step-slap sound that played its usual tattoo. Anticipatory thoughts of Saturday night and Achilles McPherson coming to sit again frolicked in her head. *Why can't we have a real dinner? In the dining room. Like a real family, with Mama and Brodie there. Why can't we?*

When she reached the backyard, she called, "Queen Esther! Aunt Charlotte! Where are you?"

"Right here in the kitchen," answered Queen. "Anything wrong?"

"You bet there's something wrong," replied Annie Earle, climbing the back porch steps.

Aunt Charlotte's clouded face popped through the kitchen door. "Something wrong?" she asked.

"We never use our dining room," announced Annie Earle.

Aunt Charlotte and Queen Esther looked baffled.

"We never have any company. What are we keeping that fine dining room polished and shined for if nobody ever sets foot in it for a meal?"

The two women just stared at Annie Earle.

"I've decided we'll have a real family dinner Saturday night when Achilles McPherson comes to sit."

"Miss Nel know about this?" asked Aunt Charlotte.

"No, but I'm counting on getting Mama down here to the table. I know she'll do it for me. And I'm counting on you, Aunt Charlotte, to make us a decent meal and not break too badly with my disgusting diet."

The old woman beamed and said, "Hallelujah! There be more than the smell of rain in the air today!"

Annie Earle wondered why Queen Esther looked dubious.

He came promptly at eight o'clock on Saturday and found her again in the cool retreat behind the Virginia creeper vines that sheltered the porch. The dying rays of the setting sun shot through the vines, casting golden flecks of light over Annie Earle.

"Solina Angelique," he said softly, "are you real? Or is the sun playing tricks on me?"

"I think it's both," she answered. "This name you've given me is not quite real yet. And, true, the sun plays tricks on us, especially during dog days."

"But that empty chair there next to you is real. So may I take a seat?" he asked.

"Sit, Billy Blue. And tell me the news from deep inside the great green swamp."

"The alligators are fat and lazy. The mosquitoes are lean and hungry. A brown bear with a sweet tooth raided our neighbor's cabin and ate two pounds of black molasses. I stepped on a sleeping water moccasin, but jumped away before it could strike. A snapping turtle latched onto the foreman's dog's tail and it took half the camp to catch and free the panicked animal. Not much of interest, I'm afraid. Just your routine week at Sawdust Village."

"I'm overwhelmed!" exclaimed Annie Earle.

"What about Vineland? Any big to-dos the past week?" he asked.

"Well, nothing to compare with alligators, bears, and snapping turtles."

"How's your mama doing?"

"Oh, Mama's much better. She's coming down to have dinner with us tonight."

"Dinner?"

"Oh, my goodness, I didn't tell you. Aunt Charlotte's cooked up a real company dinner."

There was a rustle at the front door. Annie Earle and Achilles turned toward the sound. Through the filter of the screen door, they saw a beautiful woman in a flowing lavender dress, framed in the entranceway. She fluttered a lace-edged handkerchief and cleared her throat.

"Mama," called Annie Earle, pushing up from her rocker.

Achilles rose.

"Mama," she repeated as she step-slapped past Achilles to the door. "How pretty you look, Mama," she whispered. She opened the door. Then, in an audible voice, she said, "Achilles, this is my mama, Mrs. Penelope Roland."

"Pleased to meet you, ma'am," he said, taking her hand in his firm, eager shake.

"Well, the pleasure surely is all mine," said Mama. "Annie Earle didn't tell me what a handsome young man you are, Mr. McPherson. I do declare, it's a miracle some girl hasn't snatched you right off that tram train you've been—"

"Mama," Annie Earle interrupted. "Don't you think we should ask Achilles to come in? He's never gotten farther than our front porch so far."

"Now, where have I misplaced my manners?" asked Mama. "Come into the parlor. Do come in, Mr. McPherson."

"Achilles, tell Mama about that moccasin you stepped on," Annie Earle said, hoping to keep Mama diverted.

"Moccasin!" exclaimed Mama. "Don't! I can't stand to even talk about snakes. Gives me the cold shivers just to think about them!"

"Those are the shivers I got when I stepped on that moccasin," said Achilles, laughing.

"Well, I know we're going to hit it off," said Mama. "People who get the same shivers always do."

"What shivers you, Annie Earle?" he asked.

"Well, now, let me think. Does it have to be a scary shiver? I guess hearing the train whistle is one of my favorite shivers."

"Mine, too!" cried Achilles. "Shivers and itchy feet is what train whistles do to me. Just brings right out the traveling man in me."

"Mr. Roland was a traveling man," said Mama. "At

least he was until he met me. Then he settled down. But I believe Annie Earle gets that train whistle shiver from her daddy."

"Aunt Kat gives me the shivers."

Everyone turned. There was Brodie at the parlor door, in his white linen suit, looking shy but very presentable.

"Oh, my, Brodie!" exclaimed Mama. "Well, my goodness, Mr. McPherson, have you met my son, Brodie Lacewell?"

Achilles bounced up and extended his hand to Brodie, who shook it and said, "Why, yes, Mama, Achilles and I have met."

"Met and had the most interesting talk about butterflies," added Achilles.

"Well, you do seem to get on with all of this family," said Mama.

"Now, what kind of cat did you say gives you the shivers?" asked Achilles.

Brodie laughed. "That's funny, Achilles. I was talking about my aunt Katherine. I reckon she can qualify as a Halloween cat."

Achilles laughed heartily. Mama's concerned look crumbled into laughter, and Annie Earle stopped trying to suppress her giggles, triggered by Brodie's unexpected response.

"Katherine is my sister," explained Mama. "And I must say, in truth, Brodie's got her pegged. . . ."

Annie Earle stopped hearing the small talk, her mind too filled with relief and pleasure. *This is how it ought to be. This must be the way regular families are all the time. Mama and my date hitting it off. Brodie acting sociable. Even funny. Billy Blue, you have no idea what a miracle you have turned in this house.*

And the miracle held, well on into dinner and up to dessert, when Mama and Brodie wound down like phonograph players someone had forgotten to rewind. Annie Earle first noticed Mama's eyes drooping, then the lace-edged napkin held over her mouth to conceal a yawn. Brodie Lacewell picked at his key lime pie in an unfocused way that meant he was drifting into nicktation. Annie Earle tried talking directly to Achilles, hoping to keep his attention away from Mama and Brodie, but it was useless. Mama rested her head against the high back of her chair and closed her eyes. The dessert fork slipped from Brodie's hand and clattered to the floor.

"Aunt Charlotte!" called Annie Earle.

Queen Esther popped into the dining room.

"Queen, I think it's time to clear the dessert plates," she said in a loud voice.

"Shh, shh," said Achilles. "Not so loud. You'll wake up a couple of happy people."

Annie Earle was too upset to see any humor in Achilles' remark. *They've spoiled everything. I thought I could count on them to pull themselves together for just a little while. Was that expecting too much? If Achilles excuses himself and leaves right now, I won't blame him.*

He was pulling gently at her arm. "Come," he said in a soft voice, "let's sneak back into the parlor and leave them in peace."

He tried hard to recapture the easy, warm camaraderie they had found in the parlor before dinner. But it was ruined for Annie Earle, and she was unable to respond to his lighthearted efforts. She was relieved to have him finally take his leave.

"Good-night, Solina Angelique," he said as she held the screen door open for him. Quickly he touched his lips to her forehead, drew back, and added, "Sunday next. Don't forget."

The night swallowed him up while she watched, still holding the screen door open. Queen Esther silently appeared behind her, took her hand, and closed the screen. "Oh, Queen," she cried, "what does he make of us?"

Was it the back door slamming? Did she and Queen forget to lock it? She sat up with a start, forcing stiff and reluctant muscles. Yes, she decided, it was the back door. She limped to the hall window that looked down on the back porch. Brodie Lacewell was standing on the back steps, very still, slowly turning his head from side to side, as if he were sniffing the air for a direction.

He must be having one of his mares. God knows where he'll wander. I've got to get down there and bring him back.

She stepped quickly into her slippers and hurried down the dark staircase. Before she reached the bottom, a light came on in the hall. Aunt Charlotte, in a long nightgown, met Annie Earle at the landing.

"I been hearing somebody walking around in the dark," said Aunt Charlotte.

"It's Brodie," answered Annie Earle. "He just went out the back door. I think he's wandering in a mare. We've got to get to him."

By the time the women reached the porch, they saw a shadowy figure standing at the garden gate. Suddenly pale moonlight shot from behind a moving cloud, washing over Brodie. Again he turned his head from side to side, sniffing the air like a silver phantom hound seeking a trail.

"Brodie. Brodie Lacewell," called Annie Earle gently. He gave no indication that he heard. "Jesus, I'm afraid to yell. We don't want to wake anybody. We'll have to catch him, Aunt Charlotte."

The two women labored slowly down the steps and headed toward the moonlit figure. With a final sniff to the left, he opened the garden gate and moved swiftly down the street.

"Brodie! Brodie!" hissed Annie Earle with a fierce urgency. But the tall, thin figure moved silently and steadily away. The women followed.

"Let's try to keep him in sight," said Annie Earle. "We'll never be able to catch him until he stops somewhere."

Step-slap, step-slap echoed Annie Earle's heavy footfall against the quiet street. Aunt Charlotte's tired and swollen feet made shuffling sounds like muffled whispers in the night.

"You know, Aunt Charlotte, we're a pretty sorry team to try catching anybody. We should have waked Queen Esther. This whole thing is ridiculous, but I don't know what else to do."

"Thank the Lord, everybody's asleep. Folks would think we be crazy running through the streets in our nightgowns."

Brodie turned a corner and was lost from view. A stab of panic shot through Annie Earle, lending speed to her unwilling feet.

Please, let him be in sight when I make it to the corner.

At the corner, she paused to search for Brodie and to catch her breath. Aunt Charlotte caught up. "Which way he go?" she asked.

"I don't see him," said Annie Earle.

"Oh, my Lord." Aunt Charlotte was panting.

Then, from the shadow of a giant elm tree far down the street, they saw him slip into the moonlight again. He paused for a moment, changed directions, and moved on.

"Come on! He's heading toward the old fairgrounds!" cried Annie Earle.

The two women in their billowing gowns resumed the eerie night chase, losing and finding the wraithlike figure. It was a maddening game. Brodie would stop, stand perfectly still with his pale hair glimmering in the moonlight; then, when they reached the spot where he had been, he would be gone, vanished like fox fire, only to crop up in another spot just beyond their reach. Annie Earle stumbled and fell on the uneven terrain of the fairgrounds, but she scrambled up and pushed on.

"We's in the edge of Haiti," whispered Aunt Charlotte. "I sure hope all the watchdogs is tied up good for the night."

"Don't even think about that," said Annie Earle. "Look! Brodie's turning back. Hold still, he may pass close enough for us to stop him."

But Brodie swung wide of them, and the exhausting chase continued, until the circle was finally closed. Brodie entered their backyard and darted into the gazebo, pressed his back against a post, and slid gently down to a sitting position on the floor. He pulled his knees up to his chest and hugged them with his arms and sat there, all balled up, staring straight ahead with his mouth hanging loose and slightly open.

"Thank God, he's lit," said Aunt Charlotte.

The women walked slowly toward the gazebo down the path, raising little clouds of white dust that swirled around their ankles and powdered their nightgowns. Annie Earle pulled herself up the gazebo steps and walked over to Brodie. She bent over the crouched figure and called, "Brodie, Brodie. Come on, Brodie, I don't want to hit you."

The elusive ball of fox fire they had pursued through the moonlight and shadow had become a stone, still and unresponsive. Looking at the pitiful lump huddled at her feet, Annie Earle was overcome with such a violent emotion of resentment and anger that she stood there, shaking for some moments.

God! This stinks, God! I hate this foot, and I hate this disease, and I hate having a half-witted brother, and a mother who passes out in the middle of dinner, and Aunt Kat, and Bobo Bullard, and . . . Oh, God, I reject this hand you've dealt me. Step down here, Mr. Almighty, and reshuffle my life. I reject it! I reject it!

She pulled her arm back and uttered a guttural cry as she swung at Brodie with a mighty slap. He toppled over, still in the huddled position. But his body was shaking, and he started making little yelping cries.

Annie Earle fell to the floor beside him and cradled him in her arms, rocking him like a small child. "Brodie, Brodie, I'm sorry!" she cried. "I understand now that you won't change, that you'll always need me. I love you, Brodie, and I'll never stop taking care of you. I've told you that since you were little. Remember, Brodie?"

Brodie pulled himself away and looked around in the gazebo. "Where are we, Sister Annie Earle?" he asked.

"We're home again, Brodie. We've made it home again."

Aunt Charlotte looked up at the pale moon. Tears glistened on her ancient face. "God," she called, "Charlotte ain't never doubted for one minute, so I be asking full of grace. Send us down a little luck, Lord."

The Lumber Camp

····—◆◉◆—····

In a borrowed two-seater buggy, they rode away at dawn on the next Sunday. But all week long she had plagued herself with flip-flopping doubts. *He won't show up Sunday morning. He did brush a kiss across my forehead. He did say, "Remember Sunday next." He was just being nice and polite, trying to ease my embarrassment. He won't come. Maybe?*

Bouncing along the dusty dirt road, they soon had the town behind them and were headed toward the green tree line that marked the entrance to the swamp. Queen Esther sat on the backseat with one arm resting on a wicker picnic basket to keep it steady.

"The tram train only makes one trip in and out on Sunday, so we can't miss it this morning," explained Achilles for the second time. He seemed jumpy and uneasy. "Come on, Miss Lou, give us a little speed," he urged the plodding horse. After a light tap with the reins, Miss Lou gave the buggy a quick jerk, then settled again into her plodding gait.

"We've got plenty of time if the tram doesn't take off until eight o'clock," said Annie Earle. "It's only seven miles to Bedsoles Landing. That's where the tram comes in, isn't it?"

"Yes, that's the start of the tram line. You still sure you want to take it in to the camp? I've got the buggy for the whole day. We could go over to Lake Waccamaw for our picnic if you'd rather."

"Achilles McPherson, you're making that camp seem

more attractive every time you try steering me off in some other direction." She reached over and shook the reins Achilles was holding. "Come on, Miss Lou, lay down some tracks while it's still cool."

"Besides," said Queen Esther, "you promised me I could have the buggy all day to visit my Free Issue friends that lives in and around the landing. You trying to cheat me out of my holiday, Mr. McPherson?" she teased.

"No, no, it's nothing like that. It was mighty nice of you, Queen Esther, to come with us and have the buggy at the landing late this afternoon when we get back. I just wanted to be sure Annie Earle wants to make this trip."

Achilles flicked the reins and called on Miss Lou, who seemed to need constant reminding to maintain a steady gait. "Who were those friends you said you were visiting?" he asked Queen Esther.

"I didn't say any particular names, but I'm planning on seeing the George family. Lavinia George is about my age, and we be friends for a long time. But I expect her older brother, Virgil Lee, will be the most glad to see me. We been friends for a short time." Queen gave a hearty laugh. "And then I expect Mrs. Virgilina George may or may not be so pleased to see me. Free Issues can be peculiar about who their sons take a fancy to."

"What is this Free Issue you keep referring to?" asked Achilles.

"You don't have any Free Issue up Virginia way?" asked Queen Esther.

"Not that I know of. What does it mean?"

"Well, it means that certain white men had children with slave girls before the Civil War, and some of them give these children their freedom, especially the boy children. A whole bunch of Issues settled around Bedsoles Landing, and most of them has their own farms and does pretty well. They claim they ain't colored and they ain't white and they ain't Indians, so they calls themselves Free Issue. And they's pretty careful who their sons takes up with."

"So you reckon Virgil's mother may not be so pleased to see you?" asked Achilles.

"Miss Virgilina's too polite to let it show, but I don't really care 'cause I'm a free spirit, and in my book that puts me a jump ahead of Free Issue." Queen Esther slapped her thigh and laughed. "I reckon what I got to find out is how free Virgil Lee is."

"Queen Esther, you're outlandish!" exclaimed Annie Earle. "Don't you believe a speck of what Queen says, Achilles. She doesn't exactly lie, but she has a way of narrating things that makes them seem different from what they really are."

"You mean Queen's making up all this stuff about Free Issue?"

"No, not about Free Issue. That's all true. I meant about her finding out how free Virgil Lee is. Queen wants you to think she's a whole lot naughtier than she is."

Queen rocked with laughter. "Naughty. Ain't that a nice bad word? I just say right out what I feel while most folks beats around the bush. Now, what could be naughty about me admitting straight out I got a liking for that good-looking Virgil Lee?"

"Queen, I've told you that's a thing you feel, not a thing you say," replied Annie Earle.

"Whew! I'd bust if I had to keep feelings bottled up inside. Bottled-up things drag you down. How you ever gonna fly, carrying around all that weighty stuff?"

"You do seem like a free bird to me," said Achilles. "Sort of the same way I feel."

"Good Lord, it must be catching!" exclaimed Annie Earle. "Queen Esther's crazy talk has set you off, Achilles. Now both of you are talking nonsense. Come on, Lou!" She tapped the horse. "I guess I'll have to direct my conversation to you until these two birds light again."

The dense green of the swamp's edge drew closer. Trees along the rutted roadside sported wisps of gray Spanish moss, and cattails thick with long brown pods grew densely along the ditch banks. The well-tended farms and neat clapboard houses of the Free Issues stretched along each side of the road. A Sunday hush lay over the landscape, broken only by Miss Lou's plodding feet and the squeak of the buggy wheels.

Suddenly the whistle moan of the tram train sounded faintly from the depths of the dark green tree line.

"She's coming into the landing. Did you hear it?" asked Achilles. An edge of excitement bubbled around his announcement.

Annie Earle felt it, too. The whistle moaned again. "I hear it, and I can feel it," she cried.

"Uh-huh!" said Queen Esther. "Now look who's talking my language."

Achilles slapped the reins against Miss Lou's rump, and even the tired horse seemed to respond to the whistle. "Bedsoles Landing around the next bend," he called. "Hang on, Miss Lou's finally in a mood to get us there."

Sweeping quickly into the last stretch of roadway, they entered a green, shaded tunnel that was dark and cool. The tops of the trees met overhead in a tangle of lush growth reaching up for the sun, while thick Spanish moss clung to the shaded undersides of the branches and draped downward. The dark, mysterious smell of swamp water rose in their nostrils.

"Good fishing around here," said Queen Esther as she sniffed the air.

The tram train whistle sounded again, clear and close, and the wheeze of the steam engine could be heard through the trees. Miss Lou pulled the buggy through the last few feet of the dark tree tunnel, and they emerged into the sharp morning sunlight flooding the clearing at Bedsoles Landing.

A dozen small boats tied up for Sabbath rest bobbed gently in the velvety black water that pulsed out of the heart of the great swamp to form the basin of the landing. The shore was dotted with frail fishing shacks, covered with moss and palmetto fronds, and open on the sides to catch elusive breezes. Two rotted piers wobbled a brief distance into the dark water. The man-made additions to Bedsoles Landing looked temporary and old and fragile, as if they might suddenly and silently vanish, leaving the spot in its virgin state. But some fifty feet from the shore a great gash cut through the thick green foliage, opening up an artery that shot straight for the heart of the swamp. Neat hand-hewn cross ties lined the bed of the great gash and supported two ribbons of shiny new steel railway track. Down the artery puffed the tram train, frightening Miss Lou and shattering the Sunday quiet.

After a fast exchange of all the things they had already agreed upon, Annie Earle took the picnic basket, and Queen Esther shifted to the driver's seat and took Miss Lou's reins. Achilles ran to speak with the tram train engineer.

"Remember, be back at the landing by six o'clock sharp," reminded Annie Earle.

"I'm glad you thought to remind me again. Let's see, I think that's about the sixth time since we left the house. But what I want to know is, do you mean six o'clock this evening, or six o'clock tomorrow morning?"

"Queen Esther, you're in a wild mood today. You just better behave yourself while we're at the lumber camp."

"Don't you worry, Miss Lou and the buggy will be standing right here when you get back," said Queen Esther.

"Solina!" called Achilles. "Come, Solina. We're going to ride with Captain Rushing in the engine. It's great in the engine, just like riding the prow of a fast-moving boat."

He took the basket and helped Annie Earle up the short iron ladder and onto the platform at the back of the engine. "Captain Rushing, I want you to meet Miss Solina Angelique, better known in these parts as Miss Annie Earle Roland."

The captain's big, rough paw swallowed Annie Earle's smaller, soft hand. He bobbed his head of wild black curls and tipped his trainman's cap with his free hand. "It's a real pleasure to have you on my train, Miss—ah—" He fumbled for one of the many names Achilles had flung at him. "Well, Miss Beautiful Lady with the Longest Name I Ever Heard," he finally said.

"Just call me Solina," replied Annie Earle. The sound of the name sent a quiver through her. It was the first time she had said it out loud.

"Well, Miss Solina, you're welcome aboard. Make yourself comfortable and hang on. Without a load of lumber to hold her down, this iron horse is going to take you for a ride you won't forget!"

After some preliminary shifting to reverse the engine, Captain Rushing gave three blasts on the steam whistle and plunged the iron horse into the depths of the swamp. As she picked up speed and sound, cypress and swamp willow flashed by in a multihued blur of greens. Lush foliage brushed the sides of the train, and the rank, rich odor of rotting leaves rose and lingered heavily in the air. Annie Earle felt exhilarated; she had never moved with such speed. The warm, moist air lifted her hair and blew it backward like the mane of a wild red horse.

Suddenly Achilles threw back his head and snorted, "Eye-ee-ee-ee!" Before Annie Earle could recover from the shock of it, Captain Rushing responded, "Eye-ee-ee-ee! Eye-ee-ee-ee!" Then both of them looked at her and burst into laughter.

"I can't resist doing that when the tram train picks up speed," exclaimed Achilles. He leaned close to Annie Earle's ear to make himself heard above the clatter of the engine. "Sorry I didn't warn you, Solina. It's a wonderful feeling. You should try it."

They bolted forward in a blur of landscape, and a rush of hot air spun around and enveloped Annie Earle, isolating her from Achilles and Captain Rushing. The effect was almost hypnotic. The shriek of rain herons frightened by the charging iron monster and the wild exuberant cries of the two men bounced off her protective shield and quickly dissipated in the oppressive swamp atmosphere. She felt safe inside her transparent cocoon, full of expectancy, verging, trembling with the nearness of emergence.

Annie Earle, something incredible is happening to you. Right here, right now, your life is changing because you are changing. You acknowledged your new name when you climbed aboard. You drank a deep draught of a powerful potion, and now it's sinking in, working its way through your whole being. Solina Angelique will dismount from this iron horse and you'll live with her for the rest of your life. Blessed Lord, give this new creature wings.

The rhythm of the wheels sang in her ears, *Wings, wings, wings,* and the swish of the overhanging trees laden with moss brushing the sides of the open iron chariot whispered, *Angel, angel, angel.* She lost track of time. She grew dizzy and thought surely she would faint.

Three sharp blasts on the tram whistle rent her protective coating. The tram train ground to a halt. The hot, damp tunnel of swamp air that had rushed around her and isolated her dropped away and hung motionless, heavy and still. The cocoon shell was shed. She felt Achilles' strong hand on her arm.

"End of the line. Welcome to Sawdust Village."

Still shaken and a little disoriented, Annie Earle climbed from the tram train and placed her feet on the golden path that led to the lumber camp. Through the magic portation of an iron chariot she had come to an enchanted place. The main artery to the heart of the swamp now branched in golden runways—sawdust packed lanes—that fanned out in all directions. Fairy-tale shacks made of bark-clad slabs lined the sawdust streets. Rising from the center of the complex was a great sawdust mountain, thrusting its peak skyward beyond the dark green tops of the magestic swamp cypress. Pale lavender water hyacinths mingled with death-white swamp lilies along the sides of the drainage ditches that bordered the lanes. The scent of bay blossoms faintly perfumed the heavy, moist air.

Annie Earle felt rooted to the sawdust path, unable to move, bewildered by the sudden shift from the roaring, plunging tram train to the quiet stillness of Sunday morning in Sawdust Village. She needed a few minutes for accommodation, but Achilles was tugging at her arm.

"Come, Solina, let me give you the grand tour."

"I've never seen anyplace like this," said Annie Earle. "It feels like there's a spell over it."

"I know what you mean. When it's hushed and the mill's shut down, I feel it, too. You should see it tomor-

143

row morning. It wakes up with a roar. The mill saws screech, the loggers yell at the mules, the loaders grunt and swear and sing as they strain under the heavy cross ties. When the mill is running, everybody shouts just to be heard. But Sunday belongs to the swamp. I reckon that's why it feels so different. Come on, let me show you the slab cabin where Pa and me stay during the week."

They took one of the sawdust routes that curved to the left. Annie Earle found the golden footing treacherous. The sawdust crunched and shifted about as if it still had life in it. She was glad when Achilles offered his arm. He guided her around the curve to a bark slab cabin nestled under a giant water oak. The huge spreading tree, lavishly draped in Spanish moss, sheltered and dwarfed the small cabin. The lower arms of the great oak arched out from the massive trunk, forming an immense umbrella, the tips of which almost touched the ground. Achilles had to duck to enter the tree shelter under which the tiny cabin nestled. The air was decidedly cooler under the tree.

"Michael Rafael says it's all right."

Annie Earle and Achilles jumped at the sound of a voice coming from the tree. They looked up, and through the thick, gray moss they saw the face of a pale little girl. She was lying on her stomach on a low limb with her feet, arms, and long straight hair dangling downward.

"Opal!" exclaimed Achilles. "You could scare a body half to death. What are you doing up there?"

"Just visiting with Michael Rafael," replied Opal.

Annie Earle scanned the tree for another person. Achilles laughed and said, "She calls this tree Michael Rafael. The child's a bit strange," he whispered.

"Michael Rafael says he invites the strange lady to his welcoming arms," announced Opal from the tree.

"Thank you. I mean, thank Michael Rafael for me,"

answered Annie Earle. "It's cool and pleasant here."

"Opal lives in the next cabin over. Her pa's a buzz-saw operator. I'll introduce you. Opal!" Achilles called to the small waif in the tree. "This is Miss Solina Angelique, who's visiting here for the day."

Opal scrambled down the sloping limb until she was near where they stood, then she swung down and dropped to the ground in front of Annie Earle and Achilles.

"You're a regular little monkey," said Annie Earle. "Bet you're not afraid of anything."

"Michael Rafael's my friend. He looks after me," replied the strange, serious child.

"She names everything," said Achilles. "And the most peculiar names you ever heard. I don't know where she gets them."

"Seems to me she's a lot like someone else I know who goes around naming things," said Annie Earle with a laugh.

"I got to go now," said Opal. "My ma promised to read to me. It's good to meet you, Miss Solina Angelique. I know I'll like you because Michael Rafael likes you." She slipped through the overhanging branches of the tree and vanished.

Achilles showed Annie Earle the interior of the slab cabin. It was spare and utilitarian. Two bunks, two chairs, a trunk, a table, and a trash burner with a stove cap on top made up the prominent furnishings of the room. Some pegs for work clothes and some shelving for canned goods and dry groceries lined one wall. There was a single window opening with a wooden shutter but no glass.

"Not much on decoration," said Achilles, "but everything Pa and me need for baching out. You might say it needs a woman's touch."

"No, no," said Annie Earle, "it's right the way it is. A woman would just fuss it up."

"Maybe we should take this quilt to sit on for our picnic," said Achilles. He reached for a crazy quilt with colorful patches and random patterns. "I'm hungry as a bear after hibernation. Let's get over to Sawdust Mountain and pick a good spot before they all fill up."

A short walk down the path led them to a large, open space dominated by the enormous mound of sawdust. The sawing sheds curved around one side of the great mound, while endless stacks of rough-cut cross ties lay sunning and seasoning on the other side of the clearing. A hard-packed area stretched from a clump of feathery cypress trees to the base of Sawdust Mountain.

"We'll spread the quilt under the shade of this cypress tree," said Achilles.

Annie Earle unpacked the picnic hamper and laid out the bountiful repast Aunt Charlotte had prepared for the occasion. People began to drift into the clearing—a few family groups, but mostly men. Everyone nodded or waved to Achilles and looked with curiosity at Annie Earle. The single men bunched together at the base of Sawdust Mountain. Several of them dug in their heels and scooped out nesting seats in the side of the mound. Unlike the family groups with their picnic hampers, the men carried large earthen jugs and small brown bags.

When Achilles saw Annie Earle staring at the cluster of men on the mound, he remarked, "Those boys intend to do a lot more drinking than eating, I see." Several of the men waved to Achilles; one tried to motion him over for a drink, but he only smiled and shook his head.

Annie Earle noticed something else peculiar. The colored folks were mixed right in among the whites for a social occasion. *Everything must be different in swamp country,* she thought.

After an hour or more of eating and drinking, two of the men dragged a long, rough-hewn wooden bench to the center of the hard-packed area. The tinkle of a banjo and the twang of guitars pulled everyone's attention to where the men were setting up the benches. Several musicians began tuning up. They were joined by a giant colored man clutching a metal washboard in one hand and something that looked like animal bones in the other.

"What in the world is that man carrying?" asked Annie Earle.

"Oh, that's Big Sampson," answered Achilles. "He plays a mean washboard."

"But what's that thing in his other hand?"

"That *thing* is the jawbone of an ass. He plays that, too. You'll see."

As if in response to Achilles, Big Sampson began to shake the jawbone, and the loose teeth, still clinging to the bones, rattled in rhythm. After a few shakes, Big Sampson established a regular beat. The guitars picked it up and supplied a melody line. The high-pitched metallic ring of the banjo fleshed out the melodic line and added a toe-tapping urgency.

Annie Earle was acutely aware of Achilles' jiggling leg as it bounced lightly against her leg. She felt a renewal of the sensation she had experienced standing by the picket fence when she'd first heard the footfalls of the sun god. Somehow the music intensified the feeling, linking them with sound as well as touch.

I wonder if Achilles feels this. How could this charge be so strong unless it's shared? Annie Earle, how can you sit here enjoying this contact of the flesh? It's against all the Sunday school lessons you've been fed since you can remember. Move your leg, girl, pull it away like any well-brought-up girl would do. Shut up, Annie Earle, hold your peace. Solina Angelique stepped off that iron chariot, and her book is a clean slate. Solina's free, as free as Queen Esther. Free and ready to fly!

Annie Earle began clapping her hands in time to the music. She let the rhythm flow through her body. Her legs began to jiggle, responding to the music and to the movement of Achilles' bouncing thighs. The reel gathered speed. Several young men pounced onto the hard-packed area in front of the musicians and began buck dancing. Flying feet powered by pumping knees bit into the ground. An old man joined them and started slapping his thighs in a hambone rhythm. "Boom, boom, shuka-raka. Boom, boom, shuka-raka. Boom, boom!" he shouted as he slapped his thighs.

Using the same rhythm words, Achilles started a hand-slapping game with Annie Earle. On the "boom, boom" he slapped his own hands; on the "shuka-raka" he slapped his right hand against Annie Earle's right hand, then the left against her left. She picked up the pattern immediately, but Achilles increased the speed and when one of them missed, they both broke into laughter. The misses provided the perfect opportunity for Achilles to squeeze her hands. The sensation sent ripples bubbling through her, and soon she was provoking misses and returning the pressure of his hand squeeze.

More and more men joined the buck dancers until the hard-packed space before the musicians was filled with tapping feet and slapping thighs. As the tempo of the music increased, the dancers became more concentrated. Some looked as if they were in trances, focusing all their powers on their flying feet. The spectators clapped their hands and yelled encouragements from the sidelines. A bone-lean hound rushed forward and barked at the mass of pounding feet. Achilles and Annie Earle stopped their game to give full attention to the mounting momentum of the buck dancers.

Achilles shouted, "Eye-ee-ee-ee!" and sprang from the crazy quilt to join the dancers. It was so sudden Annie Earle had the impression that he flew in a single swoop from quilt to dancing ground. At first he danced staring straight at her, with a big grin on his face. With his flame red hair bouncing in the rhythm with his tapping feet, he looked for all the world like a strutting cock in ritual performance for his chosen hen.

A chill ran through Annie Earle. *This is meaning too much, too fast, Solina. You're running with feelings you've never tried before. You're rushing down paths, using only your heart as a guide. Where will it take your poor feet, Solina? I fear your answer, but I know it in my heart. Solina never looks down at her feet. Winged creatures rarely do.*

Achilles no longer looked at her. He was now fully within the power of the performance, dancing in his own orbit, consecrated to the movement and the rhythm. She could study him without the distraction of his returning gaze. Hungrily she soaked in the rays of her sun god, basked in the joy of watching him dance, and asked no more foolish questions of herself. The chill passed and the tingling glow returned.

The music shifted to a higher key and, like an electric shock, sent the dancers into fever-pitch performance. Sweat-soaked shirts clung to the well-muscled bodies of the dancers. Against the hard-packed ground, their flying feet became a blur. To Annie Earle it seemed almost unbearable. She found herself holding her breath and then gulping for air.

Finally Big Sampson held the washboard over his head

and pounded out a coda that ended with a great flourish. The musicians cut abruptly, and the set was over. The consecrated dancers immediately returned to laughing, back-slapping, sweat-soaked logging men, wiping their dripping brows with red and blue bandannas.

Achilles staggered forward and plopped onto the quilt beside Annie Earle. "Whee, that was great!" he said, panting and mopping his neck.

"That was wonderful," said Annie Earle. "It's more than just dancing. There's something religious about it. It seems perfectly all right to be doing it on Sunday."

"Any lemonade left?" he asked. "I'm dry as sawdust."

While they sipped the last of the lemonade, the musicians tuned their instruments and settled into a long, mournful ballad. A tall, rawboned man sang.

> *"I'm going away for to stay*
> *A little while,*
> *But I'm coming back,*
> *If I go ten thousand miles.*
> *For who will tie your shoe?*
> *And who will glove your hand?*
> *And who's gonna kiss your ruby lips*
> *When I am gone?*
> *Look away, look away*
> *Over yandro."*

It was a sweet and yearning song, fit for men who were far from loved ones, and wondering.

A cloud passed over the edge of the sun, causing the light in the clearing to darken, befitting the mood of the song. The leaves of the trees hung motionless in an eerie stillness that now hovered over the place. Low distant rumbles of thunder punctuated the stillness.

Achilles lay back on the quilt and scanned the sky.

"Thunderheads are building up in the direction of Bed-soles Landing. That's where they settle in when we get rain. Could come fast," he speculated.

"And I will kiss your ruby lips when I come home," sang the tall, thin man.

Annie Earle began repacking the picnic hamper. Another roll of thunder sounded close and threatening. The sun vanished behind a troubled cloud, etching everything in slate gray tones. A slight, cool breeze pushed into the clearing, causing the still leaves of the trees to begin a trembling dance.

"Look away, look away, over yandro," finished the singer.

Fat droplets of rain spattered the hard-packed ground as the musicians hurriedly covered their instruments.

"Let's make a run for the cabin," said Achilles, jumping to his feet. "You can get drenched here in the swamp before you know what hit you." He offered his hand and pulled Annie Earle to a standing position. Then he grabbed the picnic hamper in one hand and the quilt in the other. "Here, put this quilt around your shoulders," he ordered.

Heavy rain droplets cut their way through the foliage of the cypress tree. He offered his arm and started to run down the sawdust path, but he slowed when Annie Earle struggled to keep apace. *Step-thump, step-thump.* She pushed as fast as she could along the shifting sawdust. A flash of lightning momentarily turned the path into a blazing gold lane, but the accompanying thunderclap plunged it back into a somber shade. The wind picked up, and the rain cut cold and hard through the overhanging trees. Ghostly gray Spanish moss swayed and swirled above their heads.

By the time they reached the cabin, Achilles was rain

soaked, and the wet quilt dragged heavily around Annie Earle's shoulders. They pushed through the sagging lower branches of the great water oak and entered the slab cabin just as a sharp flash of lightning illuminated the interior. It was so blinding and so close they clutched each other and stood pressed together as the shattering thunderclap followed, shaking the cabin and vibrating through their clinging bodies.

"My God, it felt like it struck the cabin!" exclaimed Achilles.

"It must have struck close by," answered Annie Earle.

Another flash brightened the dark cabin for a moment. Achilles released Annie Earle and closed the door quickly, sealing the darkness around them. She dropped the wet quilt from her shoulders, felt for the edge of the nearest bunk, sat down, and slipped out of her rain-soaked slippers. She could hear Achilles stripping off his wet clothes. Her heart pounded, and the bodice of her dress felt constricting, pressuring her heart, cutting off her breath. Her fingers released the bodice row of tiny pearl buttons, and she gave an audible sigh.

Suddenly a flash of lightning pierced the cracks around the door and shot through the slit of the partially closed shutter, revealing Achilles naked and godlike. As he came toward her, the angel of the sun lifted her arms to receive him in the darkness.

Michael Rafael moaned and trembled above them, weathering the brunt of the violent storm that finally broke the siege of August dog days.

Look Away

When Achilles cracked the cabin door an hour later, the summer storm had passed. Michael Rafael's great branches, heavy with wet leaves and moss, sagged downward, enclosing the cabin tighter than ever. The ground was dotted with leaves beaten from the branches, and the sawdust path was riddled by the runoff of the flash flood. Annie Earle watched him, framed in the doorway, a sun god disguised in the work clothes of a logger. He pressed his forehead against the doorjamb and sighed.

"It shouldn't have happened. Dammit, I shouldn't have let it happen," he whispered.

"You didn't," said Annie Earle. "The power of lightning was too great, even for a sun god."

Seeming not to hear her words, he stepped outside the cabin to check the extent of the storm, and she followed. Broken branches were strewn along the rain-gutted path, and the ditches were swollen with muddy water. The call of a gray-blue heron passing overhead drew their attention skyward. It was then that they saw the damage to Michael Rafael. The top of the great tree was shattered. Splintered limbs, still attached by shreds of bark, dangled downward toward the slab cabin.

"My God, lightning struck right over our heads!" exclaimed Achilles. "The great oak took the brunt of it and that saved the cabin."

Three blasts of the train whistle cut short his inspection.

"Solina," he said, "the tram's moving out early. We'll have to hurry."

She made small talk about hanging up the wet quilt to dry, about carefully rolling Achilles' wet clothes to take back, about checking the picnic hamper and making sure the window and the doors were closed against future storms.

"We forgot! We forgot!" she cried as they left the cabin. "We forgot Brodie Lacewell's butterfly."

"I forgot, but I didn't forget," said Achilles, turning back toward the cabin. He opened the door, dashed inside, and in seconds returned with a jar in his hand. "I caught one last Thursday," he said, holding up the small glass coffin of the rare swamp creature with iridescent purple wings edged in black.

Captain Rushing suggested they ride on one of the flat-bed cars rather than up front with him. "The engine's going to take a lot of wet beating from overhanging trees," he said. "We'll have to go slower this trip. May have some flooding on the tracks, or even a tree across the roadbed."

They climbed aboard with half a dozen returning passengers and braced themselves for the ride. The rattle of the flat cars and the clamor of the engine prevented their talking. Annie Earle pressed close to Achilles' side as much for comfort and reassurance as for balance.

Fold your wings, Solina Angelique. Don't think right now. Drift, float, glide with prevailing winds. Hold on to the glow.

Through flooded roadbed and over limb-strewn tracks, Captain Rushing piloted the iron horse safely to Bedsoles Landing.

Their borrowed buggy and horse stood hitched to one of the fragile fishing huts, but Queen Esther was nowhere in sight. When they approached the buggy, a very light-skinned colored boy stepped from behind Miss Lou.

"You be Mr. McPherson and Miss Annie Earle?" he asked.

Achilles nodded.

"Something's happened to Queen Esther. Where is Queen Esther?" Annie Earle asked the boy.

"She say give you this," he replied.

Annie Earle opened the folded paper and read: "Virgil Lee and me are winging south. Don't worry. Tell Gramma Charlotte not to worry. And I mean not to worry about you. You don't need me no more. I seen you flying. See you by and by."

"She's gone!" exclaimed Annie Earle. "Run off with that Issue boy. Do you know where they went?" she asked.

"They be catching the Atlantic Coast Line at Hallsboro, ma'am. My brother, Virgil Lee, give me a dollar to bring the buggy back here and wait for you. They got on that big train and went off, waving and laughing. Wish I could go on a train."

They drove the boy to the lane that led to the George farm. Annie Earle made him promise to be sure to let her know if they received any word from Queen Esther or Virgil Lee.

Light, misty rain enveloped them as Achilles prodded Miss Lou toward home. After the boy left, there were long stretches of silence, not awkward spaces, but restful silences.

It's strange of you, Annie Earle, not to feel the least bit worried about Queen Esther. Queen, you'll be back, and you'll come back with new power. I can feel it. No need to worry about you, Queen. But what about Annie Earle? What about you? Was Queen right? Can a crippled girl fly? Can Solina Angelique fox the gods who twisted her foot like a root to anchor her

155

in a barren spot? You've tasted glory, girl, and now nothing else will do.

"Look away, look away, over yandro." Achilles broke through her thoughts with the end of the song he had been singing.

"Where does that song come from?" asked Annie Earle.

"I don't know," replied Achilles. "But it's a favorite in all the lumber camps I've been in. It's kind of beautiful and sad and tells the story of what happens to a lot of people in our business."

"I don't understand," said Annie Earle.

"It tells about strange men meeting local ladies and quick romance, and how the men move on and everybody in the game is wondering, 'Was it real? Will it last? Will he come back? Will she wait?' Things like that."

"I see," said Annie Earle. "Are we part of that game?"

"Well, I guess all young folks play at that game. That's part of the fun. Don't you think so?"

"I don't know," she answered.

"It's just a song, Solina, just a song," he replied with a laugh. "Don't take it so seriously."

"I suppose you're right. And, anyway, the song does say, 'I'm coming back, if I go ten thousand miles.'"

Early nightfall in a starless sky closed around them as they neared the town. It was fully dark when Achilles pulled Miss Lou to a halt before the garden gate.

"Pardon me if I don't come in," he said. "I've got to get Miss Lou and the buggy back, and be up at dawn to catch the tram train for work tomorrow. I see you have company, anyway," he remarked, pointing to another buggy parked near the garden gate. He hopped out of the buggy and helped her down, handed her the picnic bas-

156

ket, squeezed her hand, and said, "Good-night, dear heart. I'm sorry—"

She touched his lips with her fingers to stop his words. "Shh, shh. Don't say that. It's an ill omen even to think it. I do believe God would be angry if we were sorry for something so wonderful. Good-night, Billy Blue."

She turned before he could reply and pushed as fast as she could up the wet garden path, *step-slap, step-slap.*

A black bonnet and two black derbies lay ominously on the marble-topped console in the front hall. The sight of them sent a chill through Annie Earle.

"Aunt Charlotte! Aunt Charlotte!" she called.

They seemed to come at her from all directions. Aunt Charlotte rushed from the kitchen.

"Thank God, you're back!" she exclaimed, coming toward Annie Earle with a tear-bloated face.

"It's high time you showed up, young lady, and stopped gallivanting all over the countryside at a time like this!" screeched Aunt Kat as she descended the staircase in a rustling cloud of black taffeta.

Dr. Whittaker stepped from the parlor into the hall. "Annie Earle, come inside the parlor. I have something to tell you." He closed the door quickly, before Aunt Kat could join them.

"Mama's dead. You don't have to tell me," said Annie Earle.

"She died very peacefully. In her sleep. Aunt Charlotte found her a few hours ago. She didn't suffer much, Annie Earle. It was cardiac arrest, heart failure. We've all been expecting this for some time. It's a miracle she held on this long. There's nothing more I can do now."

The old doctor reached over and patted Annie Earle's head, the way he had done since she was a small child.

"Your aunt Kat and uncle Major are making the necessary arrangements," he said.

"Dr. Whittaker, you've got to help me," said Annie Earle. "I don't want Aunt Kat and Uncle Major making any arrangements. Whatever's to be done for Mama, I'll do. I'll do it myself." She went on fast and urgently. "Listen, Dr. Whittaker, Aunt Kat's up to more than making arrangements for Mama. She's after me and Brodie and Mama's property. You've got to help me! Now!" she pleaded.

"Child, she's your nearest of kin," said Dr. Whittaker wearily.

"I'm almost sixteen years old, Dr. Whittaker, and I've been taking care of things around here since I was twelve, and I don't want Aunt Kat butting in. She's up to no good. She'd put Brodie Lacewell in an asylum in a minute."

"Child, you're upset. You need good strong kinfolk at a time like this."

"You're not going to help me," said Annie Earle. "I can see you're not going to help me, Dr. Whittaker."

"Annie Earle, Annie Earle," called Aunt Kat, rapping on the closed parlor door.

"Come in," said Dr. Whittaker. "I'm leaving now."

"Annie Earle, I'm sorry I yelled at you out there in the hall, but I'm so distracted with all that's happened, and with so many arrangements to get made, on a Sunday at that, I'm not myself. I do feel for you and Brodie Lacewell, and my sorrows and prayers are with you."

"I do appreciate your offer to help, Aunt Kat. But I'd like to make whatever arrangements are necessary myself."

"But Mr. Major has already sent word for Peacock's Funeral Home to come for the body."

"Aunt Kat, Mama's not going to any funeral home," said Annie Earle. "She hated funeral homes. She said to me many a time, 'Annie Earle, don't send me to any of those charnel houses where they pump your insides full of embalming fluids. It's a horrible violation of the dead.' No, Aunt Kat, whatever laying out is done for Mama will be done by Aunt Charlotte. She's cared for her all these years, and it's only fit she perform this last rite."

"You're out of your head with grief, Annie Earle. No person in their right mind would allow their mother to be laid out by a nigger. It just isn't done these days. Everyone who's anybody has their folks embalmed. Mr. Major will take care of it, child. You don't have a thing to worry about."

Annie Earle walked past Aunt Kat toward the door that was still ajar from Dr. Whittaker's leaving. She closed it firmly and leaned back against the doorknob.

"Aunt Kat, you're not listening to me. I said I would make Mama's arrangements. Did you hear that? Well, now you know that Mama will not be going to Peacock's Funeral Home, and as far as the other arrangements are concerned, I'll let you know as soon as they've been made."

Aunt Kat stared at the girl who was calmly ordering her out of her house and life. She seemed unable to believe what she was hearing or cope with the outrage she was obviously feeling. "I've never been talked to like this in my life! And, what's more, I don't have to put up with it. I don't know what I'm doing standing here, listening to such insults. There's law on my side, and I intend to use it. Now that Nel's dead, I can put that Jack Cato in his place."

She started toward the door but pulled up short when Annie Earle made no move to unblock the exit. The older woman gave a snort and raised her arm as if to strike the girl. With a quick move, Annie Earle grabbed the black-swathed wrist and forced it downward with a strength that surprised both her and Aunt Kat.

"Oh! You're breaking my arm!" cried Aunt Kat.

"I've got twice the strength of normal in my hands. It makes up for a lame foot," whispered Annie Earle. " And if you cross me, Aunt Kat, if you use one bit of legal procedure to try to get control of me or Brodie Lacewell, I swear before God, I'll kill you with these strong hands."

She thrust the stunned woman back into the center of the room and released her.

"You've gone crazy. You're out of your mind. How dare you threaten me! We'll settle these accounts as soon as I'm your legal guardian. Now you let me out of this room before I call out for Mr. Major."

Annie Earle twisted the large decorative key that rested in the parlor door keyhole. With the door safely locked, she moved swiftly to the marble-topped table with the dragon-decorated cachepot. Without taking her eyes from Aunt Kat, she dug her hand into the dried rose petals and found Granny Buzzard's conjure bag.

"You make one move, Aunt Kat, one move to become my legal guardian, and you'll end up dead." She thrust the conjure bag under her aunt's nose. "I won't even have to touch you. I'll have a spell put on you that'll wither you to skin and bones in two months' time." She rubbed the bag against the frightened woman's face.

"Get away from me!" shrieked Aunt Kat. "What's that stinking thing in your hand?"

"A conjure bag, Aunt Kat. It's been waiting for you to make this move. But I'll never speak of it again. And I'll swear before God and man that I know nothing about such nonsense. I'll act sorry and sympathetic for my closest living relative. I'll appear to grieve that she's wasting away so fast."

Aunt Kat pulled away. "You're talking nigger talk. You can't scare me with that."

"I don't intend to scare you, Aunt Kat. Not yet. Right now I'm merely being merciful. It's rare that one gives warning before casting a spell. You're lucky, Aunt Kat. You have options. Most victims don't."

Aunt Kat's hand fidgeted nervously with her face, tracing the path the conjure bag had made. "Just nigger talk," she mumbled. "Can't touch you if you don't believe it."

"*You* don't have to believe, Aunt Kat. The only thing that matters is that *I* believe. One move, Aunt Kat, and you'll believe when it strikes you."

Annie Earle step-slapped to the cachepot, thinking, *For a moment there I did believe. I think I put in the missing ingredient, Granny Buzzard. Queen Esther said I would when I needed it bad enough.*

She replaced the conjure bag, then moved past Aunt Kat, who was making small snorting sounds and wiping her face with a lace-edged handkerchief. She unlocked the door and stood to one side, waiting for Aunt Kat to leave the room.

"Kat, I've found it," called Uncle Major. He was hurrying down the steps with a bankbook in his hand. "There's more here than we thought," he continued, not having seen Annie Earle standing in the parlor doorway.

"Come, Mr. Major," said Aunt Kat. "We're going home. Annie Earle wants to make the arrangements for Penelope, and I've never been one to thrust my services on people who don't appreciate them."

"But I don't understand," stammered Uncle Major. He

pulled out his large gold railway watch and checked the dial for enlightenment. "Mr. Peacock's man is due here any minute."

"We won't be needing Mr. Peacock," announced Annie Earle. Then she moved toward Uncle Major and swiftly plucked the bankbook from his hand.

"She's gone crazy," hissed Aunt Kat. "We'll have to humor her for a while. I've had all I can stand for one day. Take me home, Mr. Major."

As the two dark figures brushed past Annie Earle, she said gently, "I hope the clawing feeling around your heart improves by tomorrow, Aunt Kat."

With genuine fear in her eyes, Aunt Kat clutched her breast and rushed from the house.

Annie Earle turned to Aunt Charlotte and silently let the old woman wrap her in caring and healing arms. They both stood for a few moments, shaking and sharing their anguish.

"Where is Brodie?" asked Annie Earle.

"He be in the kitchen, just sitting and staring."

"Does he know?"

"He knows, but he don't know," answered Aunt Charlotte. "Where's Queen?"

"Queen's gone, Aunt Charlotte. You can't coop a wild bird. Queen flew off today. I think maybe she left on the same current that Mama flew away on. But Queen'll be back. Don't worry. She's only making a seasonal migration."

They buried Penelope Anne Roland in the Vineland City Cemetery under a long low marker that commemorated two people. Mr. Roland lay to the right and his engraving gave dates of birth and death.

The left space on the long marker bore Mama's full

name: Penelope Anne Howard Roland, with her date of birth followed by a dash and space left for adding a terminal date. "Rest in Peace" was engraved on a marble streamer held by flying angels, floating above the two names.

The small group surrounding Annie Earle remained standing in the drizzle at the graveside as the minister, relatives, and acquaintances picked their way through the mud to their waiting buggies. Aunt Kat and Uncle Major lingered. Aunt Kat fidgeted with a black handkerchief, dabbing at her nose and eyes. She kept glancing toward Annie Earle and bobbing her head as if she had developed a tremor. She sneezed twice, blew her nose, and signaled her husband to leave.

Aunt Charlotte, Brodie Lacewell, Jack Cato, Achilles, and Annie Earle were left alone. Annie Earle reached down and plucked a carnation from one of the floral displays.

"Good-bye, Mama. I've loved you well, and I've found the strength to carry out your last wish."

Aunt Charlotte muttered a prayer. And Brodie Lacewell knelt at the foot of the fresh grave mound and scooped out a hole in the soft, wet earth. He reached into his suit pocket and pulled out a small glass jar. As he covered it quickly with loose grave soil, Annie Earle glimpsed the iridescent wings of the rare swamp butterfly.

"Will you come to the house with us?" Annie Earle asked Achilles.

"Of course," he answered.

When they returned to the empty house, Annie Earle began to feel panicky. The calm that had sustained her through the confrontation with Aunt Kat and the funeral arrangements was all used up. Her mind and plans were racing at such speed she felt she might derail at any moment. She was desperate to talk with Achilles. She was sure he was the solution to the problem she'd feared so long.

She calmed herself as best she could and plunged forward. "Achilles, don't say anything until I've finished. Hear me out and do this one thing I ask of you. When I've finished what I have to say, place your arms around me and hold me for a long spell—or say good-bye to me, as I just said it to Mama, and leave my life forever."

Achilles looked at her with awe and puzzlement.

"Will you promise to do one of those two things?"

He nodded.

"Achilles, I'm asking you to marry me. Not for what happened at the lumber camp. I'm asking you to marry me, first, because I dearly love you. But in full truth, I need a husband, and I need him now. I'm under legal age and my relatives are hovering, waiting to pounce on me and Brodie and Mama's estate. For Brodie and me it means being put away in religious institutions, and for Aunt Charlotte it means being put out to pasture. God knows what they'll manage to do with Mama's property before I can control it myself. Mama owned a lot of prime property in this town, Achilles, more than you can imagine. And if it's used right, we could be rich one day. Rich enough to go our own way and fly in the face of this town. The lumber business is growing so fast, this town hasn't begun to catch up. Mama owns property where somebody should build a hotel and a nickelodeon and all kinds of business places. This town's headed for boom times, and we own the most choice land around. We could do it, Achilles. You marry me, and we'll start tomorrow— Well, maybe we should have a week's honeymoon. We'll start a week from now turning this town's tired old bottom upside down."

She paused for breath, but held up a restraining hand to indicate that he was to say nothing yet. "There's a magic time that surrounds everybody, and our time has come. Queen Esther knew it. Achilles, I feel the magic and the power of its force. But it's fleeting, and it won't come this way again. We've got to catch ahold and follow it with no questions and no fears. Nothing on earth could stop me with your love and your support. Achilles, I'm not like other girls, and I don't mean I'm different because of a clubfoot. I mean different because I'm not afraid to reach for a dream and make it happen. You're the bedrock I've been looking for. Achilles, you're my love and my passport. You're my salvation."

She stopped and stood breathless with her eyes closed. After the bold statement, she had no strength left to witness his decision. She heard his footfalls and suddenly she felt his arms enclose her. An unbearable flood of joy and relief swept over her. Then he released her, and with his fingertips he opened her eyes. He looked deep within them and said, "Good-bye, dear heart. Forgive me, but I needed to hold you again before I said it."

Over Yandro

After Achilles had said good-bye, Annie Earle sat for two days and two nights in her worry rocker, touching neither food nor drink. She was terrified that she would crash into the limbo world where Brodie lived and where Mama had lingered so long.

By the second day she was light-headed and having blurred visions of Mama and Achilles riding on a tram train so fast she couldn't catch their faces. She knew them only by their hazy shapes. A single snatch of song rang over and over in her ears: *Look away, look away, over yandro.*

Once Queen Esther's face came through, and it was sharp and clear as morning light. It was then that she cried out, "Queen Esther, where are you?" In her vision Queen smiled back and said, "I be there. Just believe me. You can't touch me, but I be there since you spread your wings! I be inside you now." And Annie Earle knew that it was true. Achilles McPherson was gone. Solina Angelique was still here.

The rocker stopped, and she realized Jack Cato was there, had been there day and night, standing by, giving her a hand to hold.

"I'll be all right now," she told him, and sent him home to ease his own weariness.

No word came from Aunt Kat. She neither visited nor communicated through Powell and Powell, her attorneys. "Not hearing makes me more uneasy than getting bad news," said Jack Cato. "Meantime, I want you to know, Annie Earle, that I've quietly petitioned the court for the right to continue to administer Mrs. Roland's estate, acting as legal guardian for you and Brodie until you come of age."

"Mama put her trust in you, Jack, and so do I," she replied.

"We'll have to be prepared for a tough fight if your aunt Katherine contests my guardianship," he warned. "The local courts will favor her, and the Powells have strong connections."

Annie Earle heard Jack Cato's words, but she showed little interest in the ventures he was so eager to get under way for the Roland estate. Without Mama and Queen Esther, the house felt too empty and quiet, as though a funeral hush still hovered over it. She was grateful for Jack Cato's frequent visits. And, little by little, she began to respond to his business propositions with more than "Do what you think is best."

It was during the cool weather of October, when the chrysanthemums painted the Roland yard with splashes of yellow, gold, and bronze, that she felt herself snap back. She would always mourn Mama, and maybe Achilles McPherson, as well, but now she was ready to listen to Jack Cato.

"Investing in Haiti is going to pay off big, you'll see," he explained. "Now that Vineland is spreading out in all directions, that low marshy land between Haiti and the railroad tracks that nobody thought was worth a cent is going to be valuable commercial property. I've put out the word that we'll pay a good price for any lots folks might want to sell there. And Miss Annie Earle Roland is shortly going to own most of it. What do you think of that?"

What do I think of that, dear Jack Cat? I think that sounds very much like what I told Achilles McPherson we could do with this town. Is it possible that you and I think alike, that you're the man who'll understand me?

"I think you're sharp as a sandspur, Jack," she said. "Do it!"

Annie Earle enjoyed the surprised look her reply brought to his face. Suddenly she felt laughter bubbling up deep inside herself.

Jack Cato's surprised expression melted into a grin. "Now, this next venture moves up closer to home than property bordering on Haiti," he said. " This town needs two things, a hotel and a pharmacy with a soda fountain. Your house is set back a whole block from the street. What do you think of building across the front of the block?

"Well, I don't know. But I do like the idea of a soda fountain."

"How do you like the idea of being the richest woman in town?"

"Rich enough not to worry about what might happen to Brodie or Aunt Charlotte?" *And Queen Esther.*

"We can do it, Annie Earle," he cried, pouncing from the chair. He prowled the room, pounding his right fist into his left hand. "Give us a few years' breathing time, with no interference from Miss Katherine, and you'll own this town."

He paused and riveted his intense, black, sparkling eyes on her. "Annie Earle, would it be out of order now to ask—"

She knew what words would follow. And she knew that she would say yes if she let him put the words to her. *Not so soon, Annie Earle. There's time. This is no traveling man.* She cut in before he could finish. "I don't give a hoot about owning this town, Jack. But I'm with you all the way if it gives me the power to run our lives the way we want."

He looked disappointed, but determined. "Is that a yes to the hotel and pharmacy?"

"That's a yes."

"That's music to my ears. Now I've got some music for yours."

"Whatever do you mean?"

"I mean I've found out that Powell and Powell attorneys are furious with your aunt Katherine. She's refused to sign the papers they've drawn up to demand guardianship over you and Brodie."

"Aunt Kat refuses to sign? I don't understand. It's just what she wants."

"Powell and Powell don't understand, either. She claims her health is too delicate to take on such responsibility. She has dizzy spells and can't keep anything in her stomach."

"The conjure bag," whispered Annie Earle. She hadn't thought about it since that dreadful night with Aunt Kat.

"I didn't catch what you said."

"Oh, it was nothing. That *is* music to my ears, Jack. I don't mean Aunt Kat's being sick. You know what I mean. And I do believe we are going to own this town."